YOSEMITE Tomboy

Other Books by Shirley Sargent

Stop the Typewriters
Ranger in Skirts
John Muir in Yosemite
Galen Clark, Yosemite Guardian
Enchanted Childhoods

YOSEMITE
Tomboy

Shirley Sargent

Illustrated by
Aileen Allen

Ponderosa Press
Mariposa, California

Printed in the United States of America

Edited by Peter Browning
Cover design by Larry Van Dyke

Library of Congress Catalog Card Number: 94–67635
ISBN: 0–9642244–0–2

First edition 1967 by Abelard-Schuman Limited
Revised edition, 1994

Ponderosa Press • 5204 Hospital Road • Mariposa, CA 95338

Contents

This book is dedicated to
Marilyn Fry, who bugged me for
years to revise and reprint it. She
even helped with last-minute
changes and proofing.

All the Yosemite places and
historical figures told about
in this book are, or were, real
except Mrs. Meade. She and
her family history are imaginary,
as are the rest of the characters
and their activities. The story
is set in the mid-1930s.

SHIRLEY SARGENT

1 "DON'T CRY, JAN"

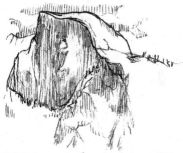

ALL DAY LONG people had been telling Jan Kern not to cry. In the blue and gold Sierra morning her mother had kissed her good-bye, saying, "You're eleven years old, dear, too old to cry but old enough to stay with the Thayers and go to school in Yosemite Valley until Daddy, Martha, and I move down too."

"When?" Jan had bitten her lip to keep from crying.

"Just as soon as snow makes it impossible to work on the highway here."

Work could be done only in the summer because at that altitude snow smothered the high country during winter. It had been the middle of June before monster snowplows had finally opened the Tioga Road, the two-lane highway that linked Yosemite National Park to the state of Nevada. While Jan's father, Tom Kern, had helped direct the repair and repaving of the road, the Kerns had lived in a construction camp at Tuolumne Meadows.

Jan had looked up at the deep-blue, cloudless sky that arched above. Now it was early September, and she knew it might not snow for weeks. Tears ran from her eyes and began sliding down her freckled cheeks. She had never, ever been separated from her parents for more than a night or two. She didn't want to leave Tuolumne

Meadows with its peace and grandeur, its herds of brows-
ing deer, and its lazy, fat marmots.

Her father swooped her up in his arms. "How can you
be sad? You and Toby will be living in a house instead of
a tent. You won't have to carry wood or water, and you
will be living in one of the world's best places, Yosemite
Valley. Good-bye, darling girl. Be good, and remember
you are a girl, not a boy. Besides, Toby's going too, and
you like the Thayers."

Mr. Thayer was the chief engineer for Yosemite, and
Jan did like him and his wife. Their fourteen-year-old son,
Chuck, and Jan's brother, Toby, were both fourteen and
already good friends. Whenever his dad came up on an
inspection trip, Chuck had come along, and the teenagers
had included tomboy Jan in most of their activities.

"On top of everything else," Jan's mother reminded
her, "you're *finally* going to see Yosemite Valley. Here,
take your medicine. I'm giving you a lot so you won't get
carsick again."

Jan didn't get carsick, but the pills made her so sleepy
she slept for most of the trip in Mr. Thayer's car. Twice
during the past summer Jan had become so carsick that
the Kerns had to turn around and go back to camp. The
next time the family drove down to see the famous
Yosemite Valley, Jan had stayed in the camp with friends.

"Wake up," Toby reached over and shook her. "Wake
up. We are almost in the Valley, and the road is straight.
You can't sleep now. You have to look."

Jan sat up, opened her eyes wide, and forgot to be sad.
She was too busy looking, staring actually, at the canyon.

"Yosemite Valley is seven miles long," Mr. Thayer
explained. "It's narrow, though, only a mile across at its

"Goodbye, darling girl, and remember you are a girl, not a boy."

widest. That's where Yosemite Village is. Our house is near the school you will go to."

"Glaciers gouged this Valley, granite walls tower above it, and four major waterfalls pour into it," Chuck recited proudly. "On your right are the Three Graces and Bridalveil Fall, and on the left is El Capitan." Chuck made it sound as if they were old friends of his.

There were so many towering cliffs and so many names that Jan didn't think she would remember any of them. "The round-topped ones are called domes," Chuck explained.

"We climbed Lembert Dome lots of times, and the top was flattish," Jan thought out loud. "How do you tell a peak from a dome?"

"That's easy," Chuck answered, "peaks aim for the sky. A peak is higher, thinner, and sharper than a dome."

Mr. Thayer pulled the car off the road and stopped. "Look ahead of us," he said quietly. "You can see Sentinel Dome and Sentinel Peak, and their shapes tell you which is which."

Jan saw that the dome was sort of like the rounded top of an ice cream cone, and the peak was high and jagged.

It wasn't until she was unpacking her suitcase in the Thayer's brown frame house that Jan felt sad again. Instead of everyone being crowded into a tent, the Thayers had their belongings scattered through seven rooms. Instead of a bunk bed in a corner, she had a bedroom all to herself. It had billowing white curtains and a fancy dressing table. It wasn't her type of room at all. It was Katy Thayer's room, but she was away at college. Katy loved being a girl. Jan didn't. She hated being a girl, and she hated being away from her parents.

Tears threatened again, but Toby came in and said roughly, "Don't you dare cry, or you can't go riding."

"Riding? On horses?"

"Not on bears, silly. Hurry with your unpacking."

Jan hurried, throwing her socks and underwear in a bureau drawer and hanging her dresses up in the closet. Rick Dunning, who was a ranger's son and just Toby's age, had been teaching her to ride horseback at Tuolumne Meadows. She loved riding.

The friends walked to the shadowy stables where the rangers' horses were kept. Chuck was tall, husky, and black-haired. Toby was a head shorter and was slim but muscular. His rusty hair spilled over his forehead. Dressed in jeans and a plaid shirt, her blond hair shoved back under a baseball cap, Jan looked like a boy too.

Carrots and stroking were awarded the horses before they were saddled. Chuck explained that both he and his sister had horses. "Tenaya is mine," he said, "and Tioga is Katy's. He's a real beauty. See?"

Toby whistled, and Jan stared admiringly at the proud-looking black horse. Tenaya, she realized, was named after an Indian chief and a beautiful mountain lake. Tioga was an Indian word too—the name of the road her dad was working on and of the only high-elevation entrance to the Park.

Chuck said generously, "You're turning into a good rider, Jan, so you can ride Tioga."

"I CAN?" Jan's eyes were wide with delight.

Just then Rick Dunning walked in, saying cheerfully, "Are you two ready for the grand tour of Yosemite Valley guided by Chuckling Chuck and Wicked Rick?" He had blue eyes, and his hair—what there was of it after a butch cut—was as blond as Jan's. He had a horse of his own, and Chuck was going to ride Mrs. Dunning's.

After they saddled and mounted the horses, they trotted through browning meadows and under pine trees while Chuck and Rick pointed out the campgrounds and Yosemite Village, with its museum, post office, gift shops, and grocery store. They rode by the clinic, the hotel, more campgrounds, and towering, gray granite cliffs with names like Royal Arches, Basket Dome, Half Dome, and Glacier Point. Even though summer vacation was over, the campgrounds were full of campers in tents and trailers.

"There's so much to remember," Jan said, "and it's all so tremendous. The cliffs and the meadows and the river—wow! Only where are those famous Yosemite Falls I've heard so much about?"

Both Rick and Chuck exploded with laughter. Even Toby smiled, because he had seen the falls earlier when the Kerns had driven down without Jan.

"What's so funny?" Jan asked, puzzled.

Chuck gestured to the right where a great cliff touched the sky. "In the spring and early summer," he recited in a singsong voice, "Yosemite Falls cascades down in three spectacular falls, upper, middle, and lower, making a total drop of almost 2,600 feet. Most years, it dries up by the middle of August and is known to us natives as Dry Drop."

Jan considered that the Valley was like a box with no top and open at one end. Both sides were cliffs, their rugged tops lined with tiny-appearing pine trees. The floor of the box, or Valley, was level and grassy and lovely, with flowers and oak trees and pines growing in it. A green river surged through it in big, lazy curves.

"Don't let Merced River fool you." Rick let his horse drink from it. "When the snow's melting in the spring, it tears along and sometimes overflows the banks."

"What does Merced mean?" Jan asked.

"Spaniards called it *El Rio de Nuestra Senora de la Merced*, the River of our Lady of Mercy," Rick explained.

"But I thought Indians lived here," Toby objected.

"They did, and some still do. But back in 1806, Spaniards explored the foothills and the great central valley of California. They camped beside the Merced River, and hordes of butterflies bothered them so much they named a creek and the whole area *Las Mariposas*. Mariposa means butterfly." Rick stopped, "Boy, I sound like a ranger's son, don't I?"

Jan knew a few facts too. "Isn't Yosemite the Indian's name for grizzly bear, Mr. Expert?"

Rick grinned. "Right, Miss Expert, but Galen Clark said that the Indians' name for this Valley was Ah-Wah-Nee, which means deep grassy valley."

"Ahwahnee." Jan liked the way the name sounded.

"Is that log cabin down by the river old?" Toby asked. "Who lives in it?"

"That belongs to Mrs. Pioneer," Rick answered promptly. "She's the real expert around here, and told me what I know. Her real name is Hannah Talmadge Meade, and she's been here almost as long as Half Dome. She——"

He was interrupted by a pretty girl who trotted her chestnut horse up to them. "Hello, strangers! Home from the high country at last?"

"Hi, Margie," Rick responded. "Meet Toby and Jan Kern. Their father's an engineer on the Tioga Road construction. He and the rest of the family had to stay at Tuolumne Meadows until snow closes the road."

"Until then," Chuck explained solemnly, "the Thayer's have two house pests, I mean house guests."

"This is Margie Scanlon," Rick said, laughing, "another Yosemite Yahoo. Her father is the Park Superintendent."

Margie was saying something polite when Tioga skittered sideways off the trail. Jan had trouble reining him back in.

Margie said sharply, "Chuck, she can't manage Tioga. She needs a gentler horse."

Jan flushed.

Chuck said, "Jan's just not used to Tioga. With Katy gone I'm hoping she'll exercise him every afternoon. Will you, Jan?"

"Will I?" Jan was thrilled. "Will I ever! I'd love to."

"Well, I just hope you don't hurt yourself." Margie shrugged her shoulders and rode away.

Jan blushed and asked timidly, "Are you sure you want me to ride Tioga?"

Chuck answered positively, "Yes. That will give you something to do after school, and he needs exercise."

Jan envisioned golden afternoons with the four friends riding through the wonderful Valley. Even without her parents, living here might be fun. She looked about, happily, then asked, "Say, Mr. Expert, who were the first people in this Valley? Spaniards?"

"No," Rick explained, "Indians were the real Native Americans, the first and only inhabitants for centuries after glacial action carved the Valley."

Chuck chimed in, "The first white men in the Valley were two American gold miners who were chasing a grizzly bear in October 1849. They saw it from the lower end."

"In 1851, a large number of miners became temporary soldiers and pretty well explored the place when they were trying to capture a band of Indians," Rick added.

Jan was excited, imagining Indians hiding in caves and ravines. "Then what happened?"

"Oh, most of the Indians escaped, and the white men left after giving everything in sight—like Bridalveil Fall, which the Indians called Po-ho-no—American names. Your turn, Rick," Chuck said, ending his explanation.

Rick grinned, "You two are really having a history lesson! Well, in 1855, James Mason Hutchings, from England, visited the Valley and then he went back to the gold fields and wrote and wrote and wrote about Yosemite. He was a regular chamber of commerce for Yosemite, and his magazine and books attracted thousands of people to see it for themselves."

Toby pointed toward a nearby road, busy with cars. "As you see, people are still coming."

"Yes," Rick agreed, "in summers particularly, Yosemite Valley is full of sightseers. Now over half a million tourists visit the Park each year."[1]

Toby whistled. "All summer long I thought you two were just ordinary chowderheads like me, and here you are Yosemite experts."

"My father is the expert, not me," Rick protested. "He's a ranger-naturalist and museum curator."

Chuck growled, "Come on chowderheads. I'll race you

---

1. This story is set in the late 1930s. In 1993, more than three million visitors came to see Yosemite's wonders.

down the meadow." History was forgotten in a tumult of flying hoofs.

Then, after some more leisurely riding, Rick said, "To our left one more man-made landmark—Pupils' Prison, otherwise known as the Yosemite Elementary School."

"Did you have to ruin our day?" Jan groaned, "It's not very big, is it?"

"No," Rick explained, "but there aren't more than about 100 students here in the winter, so usually six teachers can handle all eight grades."

"Eight grades?" Jan questioned quickly. "Toby's in the ninth. Where will he be?"

"Toby, didn't you tell her?" Chuck and Rick demanded in unison.

"I've been putting it off." Toby's voice roughened. "I meant to tell you, Jan, but I knew you'd feel terrible."

"Tell me what?" Jan's hands tightened on the reins, and her voice quavered.

Toby sounded miserable. "I'll be going to Mariposa High with Rick and Chuck."

Jan felt numb. "Mariposa? Where's that?"

"Almost 50 miles from here," Chuck complained. "We have to go on the bus, and it takes at least an hour each way. In the winter, we leave in the dark and come home in the dark. You're lucky, Jan. You can walk to school in five minutes."

"Lucky?" Jan's voice broke, and tears filled her eyes. She dug her heels into Tioga's sides and galloped away from the sympathetic boys. Lucky? she thought bitterly. It was bad enough that her parents and little sister were miles away, and now she and Toby weren't even going to be in the same school!

Toby wasn't just her brother; he was her best friend as

Not even riding Tioga around Yosemite Valley could keep Jan from crying.

well. Because their father was a highway engineer, they moved around a great deal and rarely stayed anywhere long enough to make close friends. Jan had been to six schools already, and Toby had attended nine. Usually she didn't mind starting at a new school, because most of the time Toby was with her at recess and noon hour.

She usually played with his friends rather than with girls. She liked playing baseball and basketball and running races. She did not like playing with dolls or learning to sew or any of the things girls enjoyed doing. Martha, her sister, loved girl things, but Jan was a tomboy. Without Toby, she would be lost at school. He had always been the leader.

She caught a salty tear with her tongue. Her parents were far away, and now her brother was deserting her too! It was too much to take calmly.

She dismounted and led Tioga off the trail, tied him, and began to cry. Even riding horseback without Toby alongside would be lonesome. All day long people had told her not to cry, but they weren't here to stop her or comfort her, so her confusion and homesickness came out in sobs.

2 PUPILS' PRISON

MONDAY MORNING was warm, and the call of the meadows was strong, but Jan stood outside the door of the school. She felt rebellious and frightened and strange in a blue plaid dress. After the sneakers she had worn all summer, her brown oxfords seemed heavy and awkward. She was amused inwardly, watching the other girls arrive. She could tell that all of them had to have baths, their hair washed and brushed and their fingernails cut, just as she herself had to do, in order to look nice for the first day of school.

With relief, she recognized a face she knew among the chattering, gaily-dressed girls. It belonged to Margie Scanlon.

"Hello, Margie," Jan said tentatively. Rick and Chuck had said that the superintendent's daughter would be her friend.

Margie looked at her coolly and said, "Oh, it's the great horsewoman! Hello."

Swiftly, Jan turned away so the girls couldn't see the red flooding her cheeks. Rick and Chuck were wrong. Margie didn't want another friend. She had plenty of giggling ones already. A minute before, at least the

Jan felt strange wearing a new plaid dress on the first day of school.

one-story, rambling brown building had looked friendly. Now, Jan was sure she wasn't going to like it.

If only Toby were with her to joke and tease her about being afraid. But Toby had left on the bus for the Mariposa High School after an early breakfast.

The bell shrilled. Reluctantly she started toward the door. A pig-tailed little girl, about Martha's size, raced past and tripped over a root from a pine tree.

Jan ran to help her. The girl was crying and spitting blood. "My toof," she cried. "My toof is coming out!"

Jan could see the jolted tooth hanging loosely. She reached in the child's mouth and yanked it out. Just then the second bell rang, and she knew she was going to be late for the first day in a new school, but she couldn't leave the little girl.

She took her into the lavatory and helped her wash out her mouth. Finally, the child managed a wobbly toothless smile and said shyly, "My name's Ginny Carruthers, and I'm theven. Who are you?"

"I'm Jan Kern, and I have a sister who's seven too. She'll be coming to this school pretty soon."

"I'll be her friend," Ginny promised, putting her hand in Jan's, "but I'm your friend right now."

By the time Jan helped her new friend pick up her scattered things and wrap her tooth in a handkerchief, it was 9:15. A round wall clock ticked loudly. She wasted another three minutes trying to think of a good reason why she shouldn't wait until the next day to start school.

The clock read 9:18 when she finally pushed open the classroom door marked 5 and 6.

"Come in Jan," a friendly voice called.

Slowly, Jan walked into the big room. There were a great many desks, several blackboards, and the windows were open. She saw a flag and a large aquarium, but most of all she was conscious of what seemed like hundreds of eyes staring at her. The friendly voice was saying, "Hello, Jan Kern. I'm Miss Fenton, the fifth and sixth grade teacher here, and Mrs. Jerbman called me before school to tell me to watch for you. Where have you been?"

Before Jan could answer, Margie Scanlon said is a scandalized tone, "She has blood all over her dress!"

Everyone was staring at Jan. She glanced down and turned fiery-red with embarrassment. There was blood from Ginny's tooth on her brand-new dress. If only Toby were here to explain, she thought miserably.

Margie asked, in a shocked tone, "Did you have a fight?"

"Sure," Jan answered impulsively, "with a bear, and I won."

The class laughed, but Margie retorted, "Smarty," and the teacher said quickly, "That's enough, Jan. Here are some tests I want you to take so I'll know where to place you in school."

Jan walked to an empty desk in the back row and sat down.

Unhappily, she remembered her mother's warning. Just before she had had to leave the tent, Mother had said seriously, "I want to warn you about two things, honey. You must keep your temper and not make rude, impulsive statements; and you must remember that you are a girl. Please don't try to be like a boy, because you can be a very nice girl."

Jan had only been in Yosemite Valley a day and a night, yet she had been late for school, lost her temper, and acted like a "smarty." Mother and Daddy would be disgusted if they knew. She swallowed hard.

A hand touched her slumped shoulder, and Jan jerked upright. It was Miss Fenton, who handed her a pencil and turned the papers right side up. She didn't say one word, just smiled understandingly and squeezed Jan's shoulder slightly.

Instantly, Jan felt better. The young teacher was kind, despite the poor first impression Jan had made. She grabbed the pencil and began filling in the blanks.

Except for the arithmetic test, which was a tough one, the questions were easy. She took the papers to Miss Fenton, who read through them carefully.

Eventually, sounding pleased, she said, "Good work, Jan. I see you use that head on your shoulders. You need help in arithmetic, but otherwise I don't see why you can't handle sixth-grade work otherwise. Do you want to try?"

"Sure," Jan replied quickly. Mother and Daddy would be proud if she could do sixth-grade work. She decided that Miss Fenton, with her dimples, pretty blond hair, and direct blue eyes, was her friend after all.

Miss Fenton said briskly, "We'll really have to concentrate on your arithmetic. I'll put you at the desk between Margie Scanlon and Dave Brown, and they can help you."

Margie frowned as Jan settled in the seat behind her, but the boy named Dave, who was an Indian, smiled and winked.

After lunch with Mrs. Jerbman, Jan sauntered back to school. A sixth-grade girl named Alice asked her if she wanted to play tether ball. Jan enjoyed the game until she heard the shouts of the boys playing baseball.

"Let's go watch," she urged.

Margie overheard. "That's a boys' game," she said contemptuously, but the three girls drifted toward the playing field.

The field was surrounded by meadow grass, pine, oak and old apple trees. The boys played noisily and enthusiastically. Jan itched to hold the ball. Daddy and Toby had taught her how to play well, and the girl talk between Margie and Alice bored her.

When a foul tip came toward her, she jumped high, caught the ball with one hand and pegged it back hard to Dave.

He whistled in surprise.

"Could you use another outfielder?" Jan tried to sound nonchalant, but her hands knotted tightly at her sides.

"We don't need any girls," the third baseman said cuttingly.

"Show-off," Margie taunted in an undertone.

"Catch," Dave said.

Jan needed both hands to hold onto the hard-thrown ball. In quick succession, the team members pegged balls at her. Although it hurt her bare hands, Jan caught them all and threw them back swiftly and accurately.

Finally, the third baseman said disgustedly, "Oh well, give her a glove."

Happily, Jan ran to the outfield, forgetting loneliness and school and Margie's sarcasm. All she thought of was the suddenly wonderful day and the need to catch the twisting white ball as it arced through the blue sky.

3 JAN KERN, YOSEMITE TOMBOY

AFTER the first day, Jan looked forward to two things at school—playing baseball with the boys every noon and riding Tioga as soon as school was out.

Before long, she knew the horse trails that wound through the woods and around boulders to special places. Tioga carried her around Mirror Lake, which looked like a pond, up to Happy Isles where the river chattered over rocks, and through the campgrounds. Soon the scenes were familiar, yet always different.

One day she saw a big bear, his head swinging from side to side while he sniffed the air. Another afternoon, when she was late getting back to the stables, she was thrilled to see the face of Half Dome turn a blue, almost purple color, just after sunset. That night Mrs. Thayer told Jan that what she had seen was called alpenglow. "It's like an afterglow," Mrs. Thayer explained. "Sometimes you see colors after sunrise, sometimes after sunset, but it's always a thrill."

Jan had already decided that Yosemite Valley was a magic place, and now she knew that these magic moments made it even more special. Wherever she wandered, she would search the blue sky for signs of storm clouds. She knew that heavy black ones would mean rain—and maybe snow—in Tuolumne Meadows, and snow would stop work on the highway job and bring the rest of the Kerns to Yosemite Valley. Some days, Jan saw fluffy white clouds, but most of the time there was just a disappointing, to her, vivid expanse of blue sky. In fact, because the weather was so warm, the campgrounds were still full of campers. Some of them waved to her, and she waved back. She always waved at the men in the gas station, and talked to the ranger on horse patrol. He told her that his daughter was Ellen, whom Jan knew to be one of Margie Scanlon's friends. One of the women working in the post office was little Ginny's mother, and she was always friendly. Jan stopped by every day to check every day to see if there was a letter for Toby and her from their parents.

Letters and a few telephone calls made Jan feel good, but also sad because she missed her family. The Thayers were nice; Mrs. Thayer even came in to tuck her in, and kiss her good night, but it wasn't the same.

One afternoon, Jan was so homesick that she stamped into the shadowy stables, muttering, "Darned old sun anyway!"

"Darned old sun is right," Dave Brown repeated. He was currying a horse.

"Why don't you like it?" Jan was curious about the friendly Indian boy.

"Because we need rain to cut down the fire danger. The forest is tinder dry. One electrical storm and we'll be in trouble."

"Why? Wouldn't a storm bring rain?"

"There's more lightning than rain with an electrical storm and, right now, lightning could be just as dangerous as a lighted match."

After that time, Jan often talked to Dave. He knew a lot

It was special to ride Tioga in Yosemite Valley, one of the most special places in the world.

about nature, and could answer many of Jan's questions. He took her to an area behind the museum. "I want you to see what an Indian village was like a hundred years ago. See that bark tepee? Well, it isn't really a tepee like the plains Indians used. They usually made them out of animal skins. In this area, big pieces of cedar bark off of fallen trees were put together to make um-a-chas. That's what my grandparents lived in. There was a firepit in the middle of the dirt floor that gave them a place to cook, and kept the inside warm."

Sometimes Dave told her Indian legends, and the names the Indians gave to waterfalls and domes. "White men changed Tis-sa-ack to Half Dome," he explained. "Pohono meant something like 'blast of wind,' and that was the name Indians called what the white men renamed Bridalveil Fall.

"I like Po-ho-no better." Jan sounded out the word. From then on, she liked to use the Indian names, but some of them were hard to pronounce.

Jan was riding Tioga one hot afternoon when there was an electrical storm with crashing thunder and wild, sky-splitting lightning, but only scattered drops of rain. She heard the fire sirens begin to wail. It was a scary sound. Soon she saw fire engines and green Park Service trucks, loaded with sliver-helmeted men, roll down the road.

That night Toby, Rick, Chuck, and Jan gathered in Chuck's room to discuss the fire that had broken out down in the Merced River Canyon, west of Yosemite Valley. A telephone call for Chuck changed the subject. He announced that he had just accepted the job of troop leader for the Yosemite Boy Scouts. Toby's eyes were glowing, and all three boys talked excitedly of requirements, badges, and uniforms.

Jan felt rebellious. If only she were a boy! It didn't seem fair to her that, on top of being away from her every day, now the boys would go to a meeting one night a week without her. All summer, at Tuolumne Meadows, the four friends had done fun things together. Now, just because she was a girl, she was excluded from their activities.

"What about Jan?" Toby asked suddenly, his freckled face showing concern.

Feeling better, she jumped up to struggle with one of the stubborn, double-hung windows. Toby cared! The fresh air was warm, smelling faintly of pine needles and smoke.

"Haven't you ever heard of the Girl Scouts? Inferior to us Boy Scouts, of course, but they, too, have uniforms and projects and weekly meetings."

Wednesday night, the boys escorted Jan to the teacher's house before running off to their own meeting. Jan knew that Miss Fenton and Mrs. Craig were Girl Scout troop leaders as well as being teachers. Mrs. Craig let her in the house. She was gray-haired and wore glasses, and Jan thought she looked like a grandmother. She taught first and second grades, so she would be Martha's teacher, and Jan was glad of that.

"Hello there, Jan Kern," Mrs. Craig said warmly. "I've been wanting to thank you for helping Ginny when she fell down and lost her tooth."

"When did that happen?" Miss Fenton asked as she showed Jan to a chair.

Mrs. Craig answered, "Oh, on the first day of school. I remember because Ginny was late."

Jan felt her face turn warm as Miss Fenton stared at her. "No wonder your dress was bloody and you were so late that day," the teacher said slowly. "Why didn't you tell me right away?"

Jan mumbled something inarticulate, but she was pleased that Miss Fenton finally knew what happened. She realized, too, that the other girls were looking at her. Their eyebrows went up, and their mouths made O's.

Miss Fenton began talking about a miniature Indian village the Girl Scouts were to make as a project. It was to be a replica of the kind Yosemite Indians had lived in before white men discovered the Valley.

"I can help you with that, Miss Fenton," Margie announced in a loud voice. "I've done quite a lot of reading about Indians, and my father is an authority, of course. He knows just about everything on the subject. They were the Native Americans, and the tribe here was Miwuk. Miwuk means people." She sounded superior, "And they didn't live in tepees like you see on TV. They lived in umachas. Umachas look like tepees, but they are made out of bark, like the one in back of the museum."

This was too much for Jan to take. "Have you ever tried to make an arrowhead by chipping black glass-like stuff called obsidian? We did. It's hard."

She saw that she had made an impression on the group. Margie's look of surprise had been replaced by one of disgust. Most of the girls seemed puzzled. They looked at Margie, then at the new Scout.

Miss Fenton seemed to be saying something with her eyes, only Jan didn't know what. Her voice was calm. "You must have had an interesting time, Jan. Did you ever dress as Indians?"

"Sure. Feathers and warpaint. Rick smeared that green toothpaste on us." Jan couldn't help sounding superior. "Once we pounded acorns into meal, and that's a job. We

None of the Girl Scouts paid any attention to the new girl.

must have done something wrong because the meal tasted horrible. Like old paste, only gummy."

Miss Fenton interrupted to explain what each girl was to do before the next meeting. Then she and Mrs. Craig, who had been busy in the kitchen, served refreshments. Jan thought she had done well for a brand-new member, but no one came to sit by her or called to her across the room or even included her in the conversation. She sat on a hassock, chewing on a cookie but not tasting it. What was wrong? Was Margie jealous because Jan knew something about Indians? Were they all jealous? Uncertainty filled her, as she watched the laughing, talking girls. They talked of parties she hadn't been invited to or even heard about, their baby-sitting jobs, and a bicycle trip that sounded like fun. Finally, the meeting ended, and Jan was the first one to go.

"Jan, come back in for a minute," Mrs. Craig called.

Again the night was warm and close and the air thick with wind-blown pine needles. She wanted to run away, but the friendly voice called her back. She waited to let the other girls out. Margie came last.

Her goodnight was low and scornful, "Big Chief Running-Off-At-The-Mouth!"

Jan stumbled back into the room, with her face flaming. Only the two teachers were left. "What did I do wrong?" she demanded. "Margie called me a name. Why?"

Miss Fenton's blue eyes were sad. "You don't know, do you? Listen to me. Can't you see that—Oh, Jan, it's so hard to tell you, but, my dear, at school you never play with the girls. You're a tomboy, and you're good at baseball with the boys. Then you come here tonight and tell them what you've done and make yourself sound so smart. Yes, you did. Don't stick out your lip that way. You, and Margie too, made the other girls feel dumb, and nobody likes that."

Jan's fists knotted. "They're jealous, that's all. If they don't want me to help them, okay, I guess I can stagger along without them any old day." But her voice broke, and tears rolled down her cheeks.

"Jan, Jan—" Miss Fenton started toward her, but Mrs. Craig already had an arm around Jan's shaking shoulders.

The tears kept coming. All her troubles and uncertainty and homesickness poured out at once. She did not care that she was too old to cry or that the teachers were watching her.

Miss Fenton talked to her about responsibility and not being a show-off, but Mrs. Craig gave her a hug, a tissue, and a handful of cookies.

Jan was still feeling sad the following morning when school began. She hadn't meant to sound so smarty the night before. Why, she had sounded just as superior as Margie had! Now she was embarrassed and sorry. If there was only some way to be friends with a few of the nice girls, like Alice or Dave's sister Lisa, but now they all thought she was nothing but a know-it-all and a tomboy. Suddenly she remembered that Lisa Brown, who really was an Indian, had been at the meeting, and never said a word. She must think that Jan, and Margie too, were big fakes.

Superintendent Scanlon walked into the classroom as Jan brooded. He was a big, burly man with a good-humored, lined face. "First, I want to warn you of the terrific fire danger. There are seven small fires burning in the Park right now and we are afraid of more fires flaring up because of the heat and the dangerously low humidity and the probability of more thunder and lightning. Some-times we let a fire from natural causes burn, but not if it's endangering people or buildings or goes out of control."

His grave face relaxed into a smile. "Now," he said, "let's talk about something more pleasant than fire. Let's talk about an essay contest on any phase of Yosemite history."

Dave's groan made the class all laugh. They knew how he hated anything to do with writing compositions.

The superintendent's eyes twinkled. "Don't start com-plaining until you hear about the prize. The prize for the best factual essay on Yosemite history will be a one-week pack trip in the high country, with all expenses paid.

"Wow!" Jan heard herself saying. Dave whistled, and others murmured excitedly.

"Isn't that an incredible prize?" The superintendent grinned widely. "The rugged back country is glorious. Most of you have been there, but that should only make you want to go back again. Hike all day, then stay in a clean, comfortable camp at night were you can have a hot meal and a shower. I don't think I need to say anything more. How many want to enter?"

Every single hand in the room shot up. Even Dave raised his hand.

"Good. Any questions before I go?"

"How long should the essay be?" Naturally that was Dave.

"Any length. Judging will be based solely on content."

The center fielder asked, "When does the contest close, sir?"

"All entries must be on Miss Fenton's desk on the morning of the day school lets out for Christmas vacation.

Good luck to you all, and don't forget that the research library and the museum can help you a great deals."

When he was gone, Miss Fenton said, "I wish I could enter too."

Dave spoke up again. "I just wish he'd set a word limit."

The class laughed good-naturedly. "From what Superintendent Scanlon said," Miss Fenton remarked, smiling, "I think you could win with one hundred words if the material is interesting and well written."

"That's the trouble." Dave's familiar groan made them laugh again. "Interesting. Well written. Sheer torture."

Jan didn't complain. She liked to write and almost always earned A's on her compositions. Writing about Yosemite would be fun. Perhaps Ranger Dunning, who knew so much about Park history, could help her choose a subject. She remembered that Tuolumne Meadows, which she already knew and loved, was crossed by a road and was only part of the high country. You had to hike or ride to get to other places. There were lakes, more meadows, and high peaks. Everything would be wild and beautiful. It would be wonderful to win, and she decided to do her best to win the contest.

4   *FIRE!*

A HOT, drying wind blew all the next day. Jan could see the pine trees bending before it and feel it warming the room and chapping her lips. Most of all she was conscious of the roaring sound the wind made in the trees. It was an incessant, surging noise that sounded frightening.

The electricity went off a three o'clock, before school was out, and only minutes later sirens began to moan. Jan and Dave glanced at each other fearfully. Next they heard the sounds of engines starting up, followed by trucks driving away.

By evening, thick, black smoke blew into the Valley, ashes sifted over everything, and there were announcements that the fire in the Merced Canyon was out of control.

Chuck came running back from the dispatcher's office that night, bellowing the news, "The bus can't go through the canyon because the fire might jump across the highway, so there's no school for us tomorrow. It's so bad that rangers from other parks and extra firefighters have been called in. Superintendent Scanlon said I could help out in setting up the fire camp to release a man to be on the fire line. Of course he said we have to do exactly what we're told, and if anybody goofs off they will be sent home right away."

"Me too?" Jan demanded quickly.

"A fire is no place for a girl," Chuck answered excitedly, "not even for a tomboy like you."

There was no school in the Valley next day either, since the power was still off. Jan kept busy for a while carrying wood for Mrs. Thayer's cavernous wood range, but after that she wandered around aimlessly. Even Dave was at the fire camp. Although he was her age —eleven—he was a big, tall, capable boy.

Jan's restlessness increased. If she were a boy, they'd let her help in the fire line, too. Just because she was a girl, she had to stay here. Carefully she felt her muscles. She was strong. She was tough and quick, and anyway they weren't fighting fire, just running errands. They were helping, though, and the rangers needed every helper they could find. But they wouldn't take girls.

They would take only dependable boys. The thought kept coming back to her as she started toward the Thayers' after the noon whistle blew. Mrs. Thayer was just leaving.

"There's lunch for you on the table, Jan. I'm on my way to help make sandwiches for the fire fighters. Do you want to come?"

"Later, maybe." Jan waved good-bye, resolution strengthening something in her. Lunch didn't take much time, and besides she knew she would need her strength. Why shouldn't she go to the fire as a boy? She could follow orders, and she could be dependable and helpful. The jeans she put on in place of shorts were heavy and hot, so were the high socks and sneakers over her feet. Except for her short blond hair, she looked like a boy. She tried stuffing it under her baseball cap, but strands of hair stuck out.

The mirror reflected a slight boy except for the betraying hair. She stared at it, with despairing blue eyes. Impulsively, Jan ran for the scissors Mrs. Thayer kept in the kitchen and, back in her room, began to cut. The bangs fell first. They were easy. The sides and back of her hair were harder.

Snip went the scissors, and strands of blond hair fell to the floor. The job was ragged, uneven. She ran back to the kitchen for a bowl, set it on her head and tried to cut around it. This was practically useless. She took the bowl off and snipped any piece of hair that looked long. Then she eyed her shorn self critically, and swallowed hard. She certainly didn't look like Jan.

Slowly the realization came to her that no matter how much she looked like a boy, she was still Jan Kern. In a way she was frightened, but she didn't let herself think about it. Carefully she cleaned up the bathroom, then jammed the baseball cap on her head and took a last look.

Jan saw a wide-eyed boy with a thin freckled face and a neck that was white in contrast to her sunburned arms. The boy stared back at her, a now-what-are-you-going-to-do look in the round blue eyes.

She rode Tioga bareback as far as the horse trail went down the Valley, then tied him in a grassy glade. He snorted, then put his head down to graze. As she walked along the shoulder of the highway, ashes landed on her cap and shoulders. Black smoke billowed toward her. She could hear the faint roar of bulldozers. Once, awed, she saw flames spurt up above the dirty smoke. Already she was thirsty and, she admitted to herself, plain old scared.

Despite the heat, she shivered. Fire was exciting all

The "boy" in the mirror stared back at Jan with a now-look-what-you've-done expression.

right, but awful and frightening. Sobering thoughts more and more filled her mind, but she walked faster instead of slowing down.

Not a single car passed, because Park visitors had to use other roads than the one down the canyon. She was almost startled to hear the noise of an automobile engine, but she did not look around to see what it was.

A pickup truck passed by. A startled voice shouted from it, "Hey, kid, where do you think you're going?" The truck stopped.

Jan made her speech husky. "I'm on my way to help in the fire camp."

A big, broad-shouldered man piled out of the truck. Jan's heart thudded downward as she recognized Mr. Thayer. He came toward her, then bellowed, "Jan Kern, what in the name of a forest fire are you doing here?"

Her mouth was dry. "Going to help in the fire camp like Chuck and Toby and Dave," she managed to answer. "I can help as well as they can."

"Maybe you could, but you won't." Barney Thayer's square hands were on her shoulders, turning her firmly around.

"Hurry up, Thayer," the truck's driver called. His voice, too, was familiar to Jan. It belonged to Superintendent Scanlon.

"Coming." Thayer gave her a shove. "On your way back, young lady. Your idea's commendable, but your age and sex are against you."

Jan broke into a run as the truck rocketed off and ashes rained down. After a while, she settled into a miserable, plodding walk. Her thoughts were a heavy confusion of concern about the fire and about what her parents would think and what Toby and Chuck would say, and the

monstrous unfairness of being halted before she even
arrived at the camp. That was bad enough, but to be sent
back by Mr. Thayer, with Superintendent Scanlon watching, made it loom as a catastrophe. Everyone in the whole
Park would hear about her misadventure.

Even riding Tioga, after she reached him, was grim.
Probably the Thayers would be angry that she'd taken the
horse. She hardly noticed the gray clouds boiling up to
join the smoke. Near Sentinel Bridge she dismounted and
let Tioga drink from the river.

A brisk question startled her, "Been to see the fire?"

"Yes, it's awful." Jan turned to see a bundle of bones
overlaid with tanned, wrinkled skin. Everything about the
tall, angular woman was old and brown except for her
hair, which was as white as dogwood blooms, and her
eyes, which were sky-blue and keen.

"Fire is always awesome," said the woman in a voice
that was clear, direct, and surprisingly youthful, "but this
one is due for a dousing."

Jan gazed up at the threatening, restless cloud mass.
"Thank goodness," she said with surprise, as she became
aware of the cooler air.

"Yes, indeed," the old woman agreed. "It's high time
we had rain here and snow in the high country."

"Snow?" Jan faltered. "Snow, my parents . . . the fire,
my hair!"

"I thought that haircut was a homemade job! Why in
tarnation did you cut it? I bet there was a good reason."

Her lively eyes were so compassionate and her words
so understanding that Jan told the old woman everything
about the day and about her parents. When she finished,
her stupidity seemed as enormous as Half Dome.

"Well, now that's a sorry tale and one you won't forget

until your hair grows out, if then; but come along and we'll see what old lady Meade can do."

Minutes later Tioga was stabled in a shed, chomping on apples, and Jan was following Mrs. Meade into the log cabin she'd seen on her first day in Yosemite Valley. "It's like a storybook come true!" she exclaimed when she walked into a big living room with square-cut beams and a huge fireplace.

Indian rugs were spread over a gleaming wood floor, plain woven drapes hung beside big windows, and the massive rock fireplace took up one end of the room. The walls were dark and the ceiling low, but color highlighted the interior. Bright geraniums bloomed in pots on window sills and tables, Indian baskets and paintings of Yosemite covered one wall, and the chairs and sofa were covered with a vivid gold material.

Instinctively Jan walked to the fireplace and knelt on a bearskin rug to peer at the embers.

"Stir it up and put on some wood while I make us some hot cocoa." Mrs. Meade left the room.

As Jan stirred the embers with a heavy poker, flames flickered and burned. Slowly she added fuel and thought of the good and evil qualities of fire.

Soon she was drinking cocoa and eating fat oatmeal-raisin cookies in the kitchen. It, too, was filled with flowers, pictures, and color.

Mrs. Meade explained, "This house is a hodgepodge of dear memories. Now you sit mouse-still while I trim your hair."

While she snipped, Mrs. Meade talked. "You remind me of Florence Hutchings, Floy my mother called her, who lived way the other side of yesterday. When she was born, in 1864, she was the first white child to be born in

Yosemite. Lots of Indian babies were born here, but Floy was the first non-Indian. She was always a rebel and a tomboy who wore boy's clothes and rode horseback like a champion. She might have rushed off to that fire, not thinking of danger from sparks and falling branches nor how she might be a worry to the fire fighters."

Somehow Jan didn't mind the little lecture, because of her interest in the past. Rain, pelting down on the roof, stopped Mrs. Meade's reminiscences.

"There's a welcome sound, and you'd best be on your way." Mrs. Meade removed the dish towel from around Jan's neck. "You still look like a boy, but a good-looking, neat one. Come see me again."

5 A FAMILY AGAIN

BY THE TIME Jan had rubbed Tioga down and fed him, rain was coming down hard. It sounded like a high country storm. She stood exulting in the rain for a few minutes outside the stable. Finally she walked home, reluctantly, dreading to face the Thayers and Toby. A truck was parked in front of the house, and the boys were jumping out of the back.

Rick shouted, "Hey, Jan, we were sent home because the rain is putting out the fire."

"Thank goodness." Toby ran toward her. "And snow will put out the job so Mother and Dad and Martha will have to move down."

Toby was staring at her, excitement draining from his face. "Jan, what have you done to yourself?" He yanked off her sodden cap. "Oh, NO! Oh, Jan, you IDIOT! Why did you cut your hair? Why?"

Mr. Thayer answered for her in a growly, good-natured way. "She wanted to be a fire-eater like you boys. I stopped her halfway to the fire and sent her and her good intentions packing."

Toby glared. "Jan, how could you? Is that why you cut your hair? So you'd look like a boy?"

"Yes," she admitted. "I wanted to help."

"Big help you are," Toby said cruelly. "How do you think Mom and Dad will feel? They might even be here tonight."

"A Yosemite tomboy." Even Chuck was sarcastic.

Mrs. Thayer called them in. "What are you boys badgering Jan about? Oh, Jan! Oh, dear."

Jan felt naked, defenseless against the accusing stares. Unexpectedly, Rick came to her defense. "Leave her alone, for Pete's sake. Its' done, isn't it? You're just making her feel worse."

"Rick's right," Mrs. Thayer said. "Go take a hot bath, child. When you've cleaned up, you'll feel better and look better."

Jan ran from the room. The bath water was hot and steamy. She soaked for a long time, then washed her short, unfamiliar hair, but nothing made her feel any better. What would her parents say? She put on clean jeans and a shirt Mother had made for her, brushed her hair, and looked again into the incriminating mirror. She wished it could show a girl.

At dinnertime Jan couldn't eat much, conscious that everyone at the table eyed her covertly. At least they hadn't stayed angry, she reassured herself. Maybe her parents wouldn't. The rain still drummed hard on the roof. They were coming. That was the important thing.

Once the dishes were done, Jan and Toby haunted the front of the house, peering out the rain-blurred windows. "You two act as if you're orphans or something," Chuck teased.

Toby looked sheepish. Jan laughed, but she had felt like an orphan lots of times. The Thayers had been wonderful to them, but it wasn't like having your own family. Impulsively, she hugged Mrs. Thayer, who was mending socks.

Outside a horn honked loud and long. "Dad!" Toby sprang to his feet, grabbed an umbrella and ran for the door. Chuck followed.

Jan stood eagerly, then hesitated. This was the moment she had been anticipating for weeks, yet she was afraid. Then she heard her father's voice and, forgetting her hair, raced out onto the front porch.

Tom Kern, big and wet, swooped her up in the half-dark and held her tight. His voice was husky. "How's my girl?"

"Fine," Jan answered, and for a minute she was fine, even though she had tears in her eyes. She put her head against his wet jacket, feeling happy and contented. Then they all swept into the house amid confusion and happy noise, and Jan was down, running to her mother.

Her mother held her tightly, then Martha jumped on her. And then Mother really looked at Jan and asked in a horrified voice, "Jan, what happened to your hair?"

Jan waited numbly in the silence, trying to think of a simple explanation.

It was Chuck who answered, though in a teasing tone. "Well, Martha, you know how lazy old Jan is. The other day she was sleeping out on the lawn, and Toby didn't know it and just ran over her with the lawnmower."

"Didn't charge her, either," Toby said, winking at Jan.

Suddenly, everybody was laughing except the puzzled Martha. Jan joined in because it was funny. She saw her father's face redden with laughter and happiness, and Mother had to sit down in a chair because she was laughing so hard. Her brown eyes were glowing, and she managed to look prettier than ever in a knit pullover and sweater and ski pants. When she pulled off her cap, her taffy-colored hair hung down to her shoulders, reflecting

the light. Jan's father looked bigger than Jan remembered—big and tough, but handsome with his nice, ruddy
face and rusty hair.

As always, Martha was pretty with her curly hair and
round, brown puzzled eyes. "Oh," she said, putting a
hand in her jeans pocket. "Nearly forgot. I brought you
some snow." When she saw her wet, dripping hand,
her flabbergasted expression made them all shout with
laughter.

"It went and melted." She seemed honestly surprised
at this. "But we had snow. Lots of it."

"About time," Toby laughed. "Jan and I have been
praying for snow for weeks. Not that we don't like it here,"
he added hastily but lamely, "but families are best together and all that kind of corn." His face turned a rich
shade of red, and once more the room brimmed with
laughter.

Mr. Kern put one square hand on Toby's shoulder and
gave it a squeeze. "I like that kind of corn," he said
affectionately.

There was a lot of talk about the job and how lovely
Tuolumne Meadows was in the snow, and about what
kind of work Tom Kern would be doing in the Valley.
There was laughter about all kinds of silly things. Above
all, Jan thought, there was the happiness of being together
again, being a family.

"Say, we've been hearing about the bad fire down the
Merced River canyon," Mr. Kern said. "Did it affect the
Valley?"

Jan was dreading questions about the fire. "Martha's
asleep," she pointed out swiftly. Her parents excused
themselves to put Martha to bed, and Toby set up a small
folding cot in Chuck's big room for Martha. The boys were

Toby said, "Families are best together."

going to use sleeping bags in the living room so that the Kerns could have their beds. Martha barely stirred when they moved her.

"Come along, sleepyhead," Mother commanded Jan. "Bedtime for you, too."

Jan loved her mother's low, warm voice, but she followed reluctantly, fearful that there would be questions. Mrs. Kern admired the bedroom Jan was using while Jan pulled on her new flannel pajamas.

"First time I've needed warm pj's since I left Tuolumne," she stuttered. "Lately it's been too hot and windy. Different from the high country, all right."

"Jan," Mother interrupted gently, "Why did you cut your hair?"

Jan sat up in bed and looked into Mother's steady brown eyes. "So I could go to the fire camp and help," she blurted out miserably.

After that, the whole sad story seemed easier to tell.

Jan told her mother how the high-school boys—even Dave, who was her age—had been helping in the fire camp and how she had cut her hair, thinking to join them. "And then Mr. Thayer saw me before I even got to the fire. He sent me back, but he wasn't nasty like Toby and Chuck were."

"Do you blame them for being upset?" Mother asked softly.

Jan considered. "Not Chuck, because I shouldn't have taken Tioga, but Toby called me an idiot."

"Maybe Toby was more scared than anything else." Mother suggested. "You said the fire was dangerous. He didn't stay angry."

"Are you angry?" Jan asked fearfully.

"Not angry, just sorry. It will take months for your hair

to grow out. Every time you look in a mirror you'll remember how foolish you were. I'm not glad that you went because you caused several people to worry and you disobeyed an unwritten rule. In a vague, strange way, though, I have to admire your spirit."

Jan's face glowed. "If you'd been there, would you have spanked me?"

Mother kissed her. "Of course not. You've been punished enough. Now good night, sleep tight—"

"—and don't let the bedbugs bite," Jan finished happily. Her father too came in to tell her good night, with a Kern bear hug. Worn out by all the excitement, Jan quickly fell asleep.

In the morning, a Saturday morning when no one had to get up early, Mr. Kern just wouldn't climb out of bed, so all the children came in. "What," he asked, pointing to the electric light, "is that strange thing?"

"It's a new kind of light," Toby explained with a twinkle in his eye. "Instead of pumping a lantern, you just turn a switch and presto—light!"

When the telephone rang, Daddy sat straight up in bed. "I never heard a Steller's jay sound like that! What is it?"

Toby answered teasingly, "That is Alexander Graham Bell's invention known to us civilized people as the telephone. You can talk to people a long way away."

"Margaret, Margaret," Dad groaned in mock dismay. "How will two backwoodsmen like us catch up with such intelligent children? Martha, shall we go back to the tent and live like savages?"

"Oh, Daddy!" Martha was helpless with laughter.

"Inside plumbing with hot and cold running water, too," Jan said.

"No more water buckets to carry, Tom." Even Mother joined in the game.

"That settles it." Mr. Kern shoved the blankets off and jumped out of bed. "Old Tom of the wilderness will try this here civilization for a spell. Which way to the river— hot and cold running water, that is?"

"Daddy's silly," Martha giggled. "Jan, why did you cut your hair? It looks awful."

"Thanks a lot!" Jan answered sarcastically. "I had this crazy idea that if the rangers thought I was a boy they would let me help in the fire camp."

"Did they catch you?"

"Yeah, and they made me go back."

"Oh, Jan, what if you'd gotten hurt?"

"I was dumb. It was a stupid thing to do," Jan said quickly, but her sister's sympathy made her feel good.

After breakfast Mr. Thayer drove the Kerns to their new home. Jan was silent and puzzled on the ride. She had assumed that their home would be near the Thayers and Dunnings. Instead they drove past Mrs. Meade's, over Sentinel Bridge, and down toward the old picturesque chapel. Before that, Mr. Thayer turned onto a narrow, bumpy road, dodged large gray boulders, and pulled up beside a lonesome-looking, peaked-roof gray house. It looked as old as the granite boulder that leaned against one wall. The house was set back from the road in the deep morning shadow cast by the cliffs.

Mrs. Kern climbed out of the back seat, saying quickly, "Looks like something from a fairy story."

"More like an abandoned movie set," Toby said grumpily.

They trooped into a dark living room, then explored two small bedrooms with tattered remnants of wallpaper hanging down. Somehow a claw-footed bathtub had been crowded into a tiny bathroom.

"Now I know where we can have a Halloween spook house," Jan said, but no one laughed.

Toby was scornful. "Just check the rock in the wood-box. That comes with the house, no extra charge."

Besides the living room there was a large kitchen with big windows. In two places rocks stuck right up out of the floor. They weren't very big, but the one in the woodbox took up half the space.

"Look, Mother!" Martha was astonished. "Rocks grow in our house."

"*This* is a house?" Toby said sarcastically.

"It has a roof and plumbing," Mother said sharply, "and that's more than the tent had."

"Look, characters," Dad said quietly but firmly, "it's a house with floors and walls and a roof and all those fancy modern conveniences you were telling me about."

"But, Dad," Toby said, sounding as miserable as Jan felt, "you saw how neat the Thayer's house is. Dunnings', too. How come we have this rattrap?"

Mr. Kern's face was stern, and so was his voice. "One, because there's a housing shortage, and two, because I'm new here. Three, understand this, starting right now we are all going to turn this place into a home."

For several hours, Mr. Thayer, Chuck, Rick, and all the Kerns were busy carrying junk out of the house to load on a pickup truck, scrubbing walls, and bringing in the furniture from the Kerns' tent. Everyone worked. Even Martha carried in wood for the cooking and heating stoves. There was some good-natured complaining but no more gripes about the house. The girls were to share a bedroom, Mrs. Kern announced. "Toby has the other, and your father and I will use the living room. We'll turn the kitchen into an all-purpose room because it's so big and light."

A knock at the half-opened door interrupted her explanation.

"Company?" Mother sounded surprised.

The children raced for the door. Mrs. Meade was standing there with packages in both hands.

"Welcome to Yosemite Valley." When Mrs. Meade smiled it looked to Jan as if her face had a million wrinkles.

"Mother, this is my friend, Mrs. Meade," Jan introduced her proudly. "She lives in a log cabin, and she's the one who cut my hair the second time."

"How nice of you to greet us," Mother said warmly, smiling as she added, "and thanks for being a barber for Jan."

Soon Mrs. Meade was sitting in the only chair that didn't have boxes on it. She had brought a box of homemade cookies and a jar of applesauce.

"I made this applesauce out of the apples that grow in the old orchard up by Camp Curry. My parents were friends of James C. Lamon, the man who planted those very trees about 1860. He was one of the pioneers. You see, no white men lived in Yosemite Valley year round until he came."

"What did the pioneers do?" Mrs. Kern asked. She had stopped unpacking kitchen equipment to listen. Toby was listening too, and Jan felt proud that Mrs. Meade was her friend.

"Lamon, Hutchings, Galen Clark, my father, and others, settled here because they believed they could make a living while enjoying a beautiful place. You see, the visitors who came to see the marvelous sights had to have food, shelter, and hay for their horses. Trails to walk on were needed, and bridges to cross over the river. Within a few years roads were needed too, so that people could ride in stages rather than on horses. The first white settlers worked to provide such services. Mr. Lamon raised apples and berries. Many of the apple trees still bear fruit."

"What a pleasure and honor to talk to an old-timer!" Jan's mother exclaimed with delight.

"How old are you anyway?" Jan blurted out, forgetting her manners. "Are you a hundred?"

"Jan Kern!" Mother protested. "How impolite!"

Mrs. Meade chuckled. "I'm not embarrassed by my age. I will be eighty-six come spring. When I was Jan's size I used to herd my father's cows. School kept in summer months because snow would stop us children from going far from our homes during winters."

"Did Florence Hutchings go to school here?" Jan asked.

"Yes, she did, before my time, and I guess she was a handful. She even rolled cigarettes and smoked them! Winters she lived with her family in San Francisco, so she had school all year round."

"Poor girl." Jan was thinking of how Florence must have hated the restraint of a city after the freedom and space of Yosemite Valley. Now that the Kerns were all together again, she realized how lucky she was, even if they had to live here in a drab old house.

"Is this house historic? Did the Hutchings family live here?" Jan asked hopefully.

"No, but the place is old. It was used for employees when the Sentinel Hotel was up the road. Florence's father, James M. Hutchings, moved into the first building of the group in 1864. After that the hotel grew and grew, until there were seven buildings for guests. It was a sad day to me when they were torn down one by one. When I was a teenager I worked in River Cottage. I well remember your house because friends of mine lived in it."

Suddenly the cramped place looked different to Jan. It wasn't a plain, ordinary house like the Thayers' and Dunnings'—it was a house full of history like Mrs. Meade's home or the Chapel. It belonged to Yosemite, and so did she.

As Mrs. Meade was leaving, she said, "Don't be surprised if you have visitors tonight."

"Are there other neighbors nearby?" Mrs. Kern asked with surprise.

"You'll see," Mrs. Meade called back over her shoulder before she disappeared around a boulder.

Soon after dinner that night there were noises that sounded like a knocking on the front door. "Someone's here," Toby said, and opened the door. His mouth fell open as five furry little animals marched in.

Three of them were small. All of them had black rings around their tails, and all of them looked expectantly up at the dumbfounded family.

"They look like bandits with little black masks," Martha exclaimed with delight. One bold animal put his front paws up on the little girl's jeans and made a chirring sound. "Oh, Mother," Martha cried, "it's hungry, you can tell. Can we feed them?"

"No." It was Mr. Kern who answered. "All of them are raccoons. They're appealing little rascals, but we can't feed them because they're wild animals. They should eat nuts and berries, not people food."

"Besides that," Toby added, "if we feed this tribe they will come every night and bring all their family and friends."

"No wonder Mrs. Meade said we might have visitors," Mrs. Kern recalled. "Raccoons really are our nearest neighbors."

Jan didn't know which was the cutest, the little bandits with their beseeching expressions or her sister. Martha's face glowed with wonder.

Mr. Kern broke the spell by gently but firmly pushing the raccoons outside with a broom. "Goodbye, you pests. I bet the last people who lived in this house fed them, but we won't."

Jan was disappointed but thrilled. The raccoons' visit, and Martha's reaction to them, seemed like mountain magic.

6 PROBATION

AT SCHOOL the next day, the girls in Jan's room made a great fuss about her shorn hair. "Imagine you thinking you could help in the fire camp!" Margie was scornful. "What a show-off!"

Jan's face burned with shame, and her hands tightened in anger, but she comforted herself by thinking that, at least, Martha had a good start in school. Earlier, Martha had clung to Jan's hand when they had gone into her classroom.

"So you're Martha Kern." Mrs. Craig's smile had been warm and encouraging. "Jan told us about you, and we're glad to have you here. Maybe you can tell the children about Tuolumne Meadows in the snow?"

Martha had responded to the friendly greeting shyly. "It's colder'n Greenland," she said, and Jan knew she was mimicking Daddy.

Mrs. Craig had winked, and Jan had left knowing that Mrs. Craig would be Martha's friend. At noon, Jan had lunch with her. Now that the family lived about a mile from the school, they brought lunches.

"They think I can play baseball, too," the little girl explained excitedly, "just because I'm your sister."

"They?" Jan questioned.

"Ginny and all my friends," Martha waved airily. "They sure like you, Jan."

"Hey, Jan," Dave yelled, "come on!"

Martha's eyes were wide. "That's Dave, isn't it? Is he an honest-to-goodness Indian?"

Jan laughed at the round-eyed wonder in Martha's expression. "Sure, and right now he's an honest-to-goodness baseball player too. Do you want to watch the game?"

Half the school seemed to be watching. Jan kept glancing at Martha to see if she was all right. She stood alone and yelled loudly when Jan was up at bat. Someone else yelled too. It was Margie Scanlon.

"Who's the new boy on your team, Dave? The one with the butch haircut?" The laughter hurt Jan as much as the taunt.

She struck out. In her anger, she swung the bat at everything thrown at her and went down on three strikes. Miserably, she walked back to the bench, not caring that the day was crisp and blue.

"Better call the tomboy back, Dave," Margie shouted. "That new boy's no good."

"Leave my sister alone." Jan heard Martha's angry voice, and started toward her. Martha's round face was furious. "Jan isn't a boy, and you're mean to tease her."

Margie retreated with a look of consternation. "Well, for— Are you *really* Jan's sister? You don't look like her."

"I look like myself, that's why. Come on, Jan."

Meekly, Jan followed her indignant sister. Behind her, she heard Margie say wonderingly, "Why, she's a cute little thing, not a spitfire like Jan."

"Don't let her worry you," Martha told Jan as the bell rang. "She's just stuck-up and jealous because she can't play ball."

"Leave my sister alone!" Martha was furious.

Smiling to herself, Jan decided that she didn't need to worry about Martha taking care of herself. She saw her go off arm in arm with two little girls. She had friends already. The thought plagued Jan. All of *her* friends were boys. Martha didn't play baseball. Was that what made the difference? Jan stared unseeingly at her geography book. She was a tomboy; Martha wasn't. She did dumb things that led to trouble; Martha didn't. She was homely, with freckles and straight hair, what there was of it; Martha was pretty and sweet. She was——

"JAN!" Miss Fenton's voice was sharp. "Wake up! I've called you three times. What can you tell us about Russia?"

"It's big," Jan said blankly, her mind still on the contrast between sisters, "and it's cold."

Even Dave joined the general laughter. Jan sat numbly until she heard Margie's sarcastic whisper, "How dumb can you be?" That was too much. All of her bewilderment and worry were swept aside by a choking anger.

"So I'm dumb, Marjorie Scanlon. What makes you think you're so darned smart?" She was out of her seat, though Dave tried to pull her back. "Leave me alone," she said wildly. "She is dumb, stupid——"

Miss Fenton gripped Jan by the shoulders, her voice hard. "*That's enough!* Go into the office and stay there until I come."

Jan slammed the door as hard as she could and walked defiantly past the office and went outdoors. Miss Fenton couldn't tell her what to do. Suddenly weak, after her outburst, Jan leaned against an oak tree. Miss Fenton was the teacher. She would tell Mother and Daddy, and they would never, never understand why Jan had lost her temper. First her hair and the business about the fire, and

now this. And they had only been here for two days. They
would be furious.

When the bell rang and homebound children streamed
out, Jan shrank behind the tree. "Jan!" Miss Fenton spotted
her from the office window. "Come in here immediately!"

Reluctantly, rebelliously, Jan scuffed in. "That was a
disgraceful scene," Miss Fenton began calmly, but in a
cold, stern voice. "I can't understand what possessed you.
You are eleven years old, not six. What is your trouble?"

"I don't know."

"Did the girls tease you about your short hair?"

"Yes," Jan confessed miserably. "Especially Margie. I
hate her!"

"That kind of talk leads to trouble."

"Trouble for her, not me. I'm not taking anything more
from her majesty."

Miss Fenton stood up. "There will be no more scenes
between you two, Jan. If there are I will have to talk to
your parents. I would now, but they have just arrived, and
I thought maybe you would settle down and be happier
now because you're with your family again."

"I am, I will," Jan promised quickly, "you won't need
to tell them ever."

"I hope not, but you are on probation. That means no
more trouble from you. No more fights. No more back
talk. Do you understand?"

"I won't forget." Jan turned and ran out of the school.
Her steps slowed as she realized she didn't want to go
home until she calmed down. She visited Tioga briefly,
leaning her head against the horse who nickered as if
asking "What's wrong?" Next she wandered through the
cemetery. Usually she raced through it or rode around it.
This time she walked slowly down a row of headstones,

reading the names. Effie Crippen, George Fiske, Galen Clark. Why, Mr. Clark had been the first guardian of Yosemite! There was a book about him in the school library. James C. Lamon. He was the pioneer Mrs. Meade had told them about. It was apples from his trees that Mrs. Meade had used to make applesauce. The orchard near the playing field at school had been planted by Florence Hutchings' father.

Jan noticed a tiny headstone with faint lettering. She knelt on the ground to study the name. George Anderson. Why, he was the first man to climb up the steep, slippery back of Half Dome! He was the man who put up the first cable, so that other people could climb safely. He was famous, and all he had to remember him was this insignificant little marker! She looked up at Half Down towering above the Valley. Half Dome, she decided, was George Anderson's real monument. Her mouth opened with surprise as she realized that the cemetery was full of human history.

Next she walked past a long row of wooden markers above the graves of the native Americans. It was the Indians who had been the real pioneers in Yosemite. Several people named Brown were buried there, and Jan wondered if Dave was related to any of them.

A gray squirrel with a fluffy, wavy tail ran across the pine needles in front of her. A noisy bird squawked from the ponderosa pine above her. Rick had explained that there were two kinds of jays in the Park. One was the blue-and-white Scrub jay, and the other, more common one, was a Steller's jay. Jan watched the saucy bird with a blackish crest on the top of its vivid blue head, and knew it was a Steller's jay. She forgot her troubles. Only nature and history seemed real.

As she passed a large, triangular-shaped granite rock, she stopped. The worn, chiseled names seemed to leap out. James M. Hutchings was the name on the boulder. There were other names, but to Jan the important one was Florence Hutchings, "died September 26, 1881. Aged 17."

Seventeen! How did she die? Where? Mrs. Meade would know. Poor Florence. Jan left the graveyard. But before she could go see Mrs. Meade she had to pass the big Visitor Center. Never before had it interested her, but now she entered eagerly. The historical exhibits drew her. There were Indian baskets and hotel registers and lots of pictures of people. Could she guess which was Florence Hutchings' face? Jan wondered.

One picture was of a young girl who had dark hair parted in the middle. Her eyebrows were thick and dark, and her eyes were rebellious. She had a sad, almost sullen expression. I bet that's Florence, Jan thought.

"Why, hello, Jan." Ranger-naturalist Mr. Dunning stopped beside her. "Looking at Florence Hutchings? Did you know there is a mountain named after her? Mount Florence."

"Really? Where is it?"

"Between Mount Maclure and Mount Lyell. You can see it well from Glacier Point."

"Is there a book about her?" Jan wanted to know.

"No, but several histories of Yosemite mention her because she was such a flamboyant girl." Noting Jan's puzzled expression, Ranger Dunning added. "Flamboyant means extravagant, a person who stands out."

Jan thought about it, then said, "Like a Steller's jay?"

"Absolutely," he said. "Brilliant, lurid. By the way, young lady, you and that horse really get around. Everywhere I go people seem to know you. Rangers, Mrs.

Meade, the men at the gas station, and even clerks in the store."

Jan had waved and talked to many different people during her rides on Tioga and when Mrs. Thayer had sent her to the store. "I guess they do," she agreed, feeling pleased.

"I think you're just the girl to help our hospital fund-raising committee. I'm chairman. Our Yosemite hospital is so crowded that it needs another wing. Will you help raise money by talking to your friends?"

"I'll try." Jan was hesitant, surprised and pleased to be singled out.

"Fine. Of course, we won't ask Park visitors, just people who live here. Come in and see me about all the facts tomorrow. My office is upstairs in the building next door."

She walked away, happily. She had friends, grown-up ones anyway, and she had two projects. One was to help raise money for the hospital, and the other one was to find out more about Florence Hutchings! It was almost dark, but she made one more stop before going home.

Mrs. Meade answered Jan's knock. "Come in, come in. I expect you smelled the oatmeal cookies I just took out of the oven."

Jan protested. "I really came to ask you some questions."

"Well, while I'm answering them, you can eat cookies."

Not even the wonderful smells and the warmth of the kitchen diverted Jan. Her idea burst out. "You heard about that historical essay contest? What do you think about my writing about Florence Hutchings? She was different from most girls. Maybe I could call my essay 'Yosemite Tomboy.'"

"Sounds like a fine idea. The research library files have

some information on her life, and I recollect a little that my parents told me. There was another Yosemite Tomboy, too. Her stepfather ran the Sentinel Hotel after the Hutchings did, and she and her three sisters grew up in the Valley. Her name was Fannie Crippen, but for several years she called herself 'Frankie' or 'Frank.' She even signed her name that way. She could ride a horse bareback like an Indian and climb rocks like a mountain goat. I was a tomboy too, for a while, but nothing like Fannie or Florence."

"Maybe I could put her in my essay too, and call it 'Yosemite Tomboys.' Would you help me?"

"Of course I will, child. Over here on the wall is a picture of the Crippen sisters. The one named Effie died when she was only fourteen."

"I remember seeing her grave in the cemetery."

"Yes, she was buried there six weeks before Floy Hutchings was. Floy, by the way, was Florence's nickname. Anyway, my mother told me that the two girls were good friends. Poor Floy stood beside Effie's coffin at the funeral, singing 'Safe in the Arms of Jesus.'"

Even though more than one hundred years had passed since that tragic scene, Jan felt sad. "How did she die?"

"From cutting an artery in her foot on broken glass while she was wading in Mirror Lake. She lost too much blood, and there was no doctor here, and the poor girl got weaker and weaker, then died."

"Litterbugs even then!" Jan was disgusted.

"People don't change much. Say, young one, you had best light for home. Here's a bag of cookies besides the ones you were too excited to eat."

At the dinner table, Jan told her family about the cemetery, Mrs. Meade, and her new projects. She talked fast partly because she was excited, and partly because she didn't want Martha to mention school or Margie. The trouble there was like a bad dream, and she didn't want her parents to know. They didn't think she should lose her temper, no matter what the reason. She remembered that she was on probation at school, and knew she mustn't make another scene.

Hours later she was pulled from sleep by her father's quiet voice and his gentle squeeze of her shoulder. "Jan, dear, wake up."

"There's something you need to see." He led her into the big front room, which was criss-crossed by moonbeams.

Mother and Toby made room for Jan to stand beside them at the window. "Look," they whispered in unison. In wonder, Jan looked outside, then shivered, partly with cold and partly with awe. Five deer were circling each other in the bright moonlight, heads up and alert, hooves prancing. "Magic!" Jan whispered, watching every carefree move.

Moments later, the deer ran off between the boulders and trees, and the family returned to their beds, but Jan never forgot that magic time.

7 MRS. MEADE'S MEMORIES

AT 9:01 the following morning, Miss Fenton addressed the fifth- and sixth-graders: "While you're all wide awake and invigorated from the cold outside, I want you each to write a news article. It can be on any newsworthy subject, but make it interesting enough for a newspaper. You may have forty-five minutes to work."

Dave's groan was loudest of a low chorus. Jan reached for paper eagerly, searching her mind for a subject. Horses? No. The recent fire in the canyon? She didn't know enough. Sports? Maybe. She remembered the football game between the Yosemite eighth-grade boys and the Mariposa High School freshman team. That had been exciting, and she had watched it and could describe what happened.

Miss Fenton stopped them after forty-five minutes. "Thank goodness," Dave groaned again.

"You may read yours aloud, Dave, and let us judge if it's so bad."

The class laughed at his astonishment, then listened to his article about fire fighting. Most of it was about equipment and where the fire fighters came from.

Most of the other articles were dull too. Margie's was interesting. It was about a skunk that ran into the rangers' clubhouse and how it was captured. Toward the end, Jan thought it was too full of what the rangers had said instead of what they had done.

When Jan was called on, she began with "Mariposa High hit a new low Saturday, October 25th, when they lost 14 to 21 against the inexperienced but hard-charging Yosemite team."

When she finished, Miss Fenton commented, "That was extremely interesting and well written, Jan." Jan glowed with pleasure. Margie scowled. Other articles were read.

"After hearing how you all write," Miss Fenton said, "you should be able to elect a capable editorial staff for the fifth- and sixth-grade newspaper. In other words, don't vote for your best friend but for the person whose article you liked best. May I have a nomination for editor?"

Alice nominated Margie; Dave nominated Jan. Margie won seventeen to thirteen. Jan tried not to show her disappointment. There were other jobs she would like just as well. Just being on a newspaper would be fun.

Alice and Jan were nominated for assistant editor. Again Jan lost seventeen to thirteen. Alice's article had been one of the poorest read. Disappointment rose in Jan. She looked around, then counted heads. There were twelve boys and eighteen girls in the room. Since she had been voting for herself, the count had come out thirteen to seventeen. It was boys against girls. She slumped down in her seat and wasn't a bit surprised when she wasn't elected a reporter.

Miss Fenton spoke up firmly. "I don't think you are voting for ability. The next post is sports editor. Think hard before you vote to fill it."

Dave was nominated. He jumped to his feet. "I refuse

Margie won the election 17 to 13.

the nomination. I nominate Jan Kern because she has the best qualifications for the job."

Margie nominated a girl friend of hers who didn't know the difference between football and baseball, Jan thought bitterly. Jan lost seventeen to thirteen. It seemed hard to breathe. Something seemed to stick in her throat. Why did the girls hate her? She remembered Miss Fenton and Mrs. Craig warning her not to be a tomboy, not to show off. Was that why they disliked her?

Miss Fenton's expression and voice were stern. "In a democracy like America, people vote as they please, but sometimes an election is 'rigged' or unfair. I am not happy about the way you voted today."

Three girls bent to retie their shoelaces. Faces frowned intently. Jan tried to swallow, but the lump in her throat stopped her. She doubted if she could ever be happy again.

That afternoon, after talking to Ranger Dunning about the hospital, she re-examined the picture of Florence Hutchings. *She* looked unhappy too. Had other girls been unfair to her?

She rode Tioga across the Valley to Mrs. Meade's, dismounted, tied the horse, and answered the old lady's invitation by going in. "Please tell me some more about Fannie Crippen," she asked, settling herself before the fireplace with, as usual, a cookie to eat.

"Well, I recollect my mother telling me that Fannie wore out her shoes while she was climbing Half Dome. Another time hotel guests clapped for her when she was thrown from her horse and landed on her feet without a complaint."

"And she called herself Frankie?"

"For a while she did, but then she became a gracious young lady. My mother told me that when President Ulysses S. Grant visited Yosemite Valley, he chose Fannie to walk with him because she was so charming."

Mrs. Meade looked at Jan shrewdly. "Being a tomboy is a phase with lots of girls. Most of them grow out of it. Florence didn't really mature, and my mother said she was unhappy."

Jan sighed. "I always wanted to be a boy." Her thoughts came out in slow, troubled speech. "When I was little, Daddy told me if I could kiss my elbow I would turn into a boy. I nearly broke my neck and arms trying. Being a tomboy doesn't work very well either."

"Of course not, because you are really a very sweet and likable girl."

Armed with Mrs. Meade's words and an apple for Tioga, Jan returned to the stable. She talked to the horse while she rode. "Girls are unfair and mean," she told him. "I still think I'd rather be a boy."

Cold autumn days merged into freezing nights. Ice splintered beneath Jan's feet as she and Martha walked to school. Snow fell. Ice skimmed the river. The skating rink, next to Lamon's old apple orchard, froze, and Mrs. Kern began teaching Jan and Martha to ice-skate.

Jan's afternoons were packed with activities. Sometimes she rode Tioga, with frequent stops to talk to people who lived in Yosemite Valley about the hospital's need for money. Many afternoons she ice-skated, growing proficient and fast. Other afternoons, and on Saturday mornings, she worked in the research library, making notes about Florence Hutchings and Fannie Crippen.

Ranger Dunning helped her. He brought her boxes full

of material on Yosemite pioneers. "What you are doing is research," he explained. "You are searching or reading all this material to find facts about your subjects. Write those facts down and tell where you found the fact."

So Jan headed a piece of notebook paper "Florence Hutchings" and began writing down every bit of information she found. There wasn't very much. There was a lot of material about the four Crippen sisters because Fannie had written a long story about them after she had grown up.

Neither tomboy seemed real until Ranger Dunning showed her a massive old hotel register with pages and pages of names and comments by guests. To Jan it was boring research. Sometimes the handwriting was difficult to read, and the names were meaningless. All of a sudden she saw the name James M. Hutchings, and that made her sit up straighter. Later she found Frank Crippen, and knew from what Mrs. Meade had told her that it was tomboy Fannie, not a boy at all.

Best of all, on the page for September 11, 1874, she found Florence Hutchings' name! In scrawly, childish writing she had written that Yosemite was "Beautiful . . . wonderful beyond comprehension."

Jan's eyes and mouth made three O's of amazement. That was Florence's handwriting! Those words, a whole paragraph, told how she felt. Jan did some quick figuring. Why, Floy had been only a year younger than Jan when she had written those words! Like Jan, she had felt that Yosemite was beautiful and awesome, and that she was lucky to live there.

On another page ten people had signed their names after, it said, returning from a camping trip to the high country. Florence Hutchings was in the group, along with her father and grandmother. Someone had written that all ten "came back with sunburnt noses and happy as larks."

After that, Jan felt as if "Frank" and Florence were real, and were her friends because they thought and felt as she did. When she looked up at Half Dome, she would think of Florence being the first child, and only the thirteenth person, to climb to the top of Half Dome after George Anderson had put up the rope cable that everyone had to hang onto to make the scary climb. Sometimes Jan would even talk out loud to Florence, saying, "You were lucky to live in Yosemite, and so am I."

"How can I research Mrs. Meade's family, the Talmadges, when there's almost nothing to search?" Jan returned three Yosemite history books and the M and T boxes to Ranger Dunning's desk. "There's nothing in any of these, and I want to put Mrs. Meade in my essay and surprise her. She was a Yosemite tomboy too."

"Samuel Talmadge was not famous enough for much mention, I guess. Look under 'Laborers.' And, Jan, you might try doing some original research."

"What's that?"

"Why, interview Mrs. Meade about herself and her family. That's about as close to the original, or first, source as you can get. Write everything down carefully, and I will make a copy for the history files."

"I've been doing original research for weeks then," Jan told him, smiling with pleasure. "I've asked Mrs. Meade about a million questions, and, lately, I've been writing down what she said."

"Good girl." He patted her shoulder approvingly. "I don't know what your essay is going to sound like, but it'll certainly be well documented."

"What does 'documented' mean?"

"Look it up in the dictionary, and we'll both know."

When Jan reached Mrs. Meade's house, she called cheerfully, "Hello, Mrs. Documentation. I need to know facts about your father today. Do you have anything like letters or diaries for supporting evidence or documentation?"

"Land o' Goshen, child, you sound like you just swallowed a dictionary. I know what you mean, though. If you want written records to back up my memories, I have lots of father's old account books, letters, and a log he kept on his work. You know he wasn't famous."

"Maybe not, but he was a Yosemite pioneer."

"That he was, and much of the work he did helped improve the Valley. I recollect one time——"

Jan started writing.

After that, when Jan's mother asked, "Why don't you bring some of your friends home with you after school, dear?" Jan could answer honestly, "Too busy with Mrs. Meade."

"Well how about having a skating party next weekend? You could ask five or six girls. Wouldn't that be fun?"

"I have to start writing my essay," Jan excused herself. "Besides, I'd rather ask boys."

Mrs. Kern sighed. "Don't you have any girl friends?"

"I don't have time," Jan answered defensively.

"You can always talk to me about your problems," Mother said gently. After that, Jan was conscious that Mother watched her with concern.

One morning Miss Fenton announced, "Today I want you to write a composition. It will be good practice for the

historical essay contest. How many of you have begun
work on one?"

Only four hands shot up—Margie's, Jan's, Alice's, and
Dave's.

"Is that all? Better get busy, class. December has begun,
and the closing date is the beginning of Christmas vacation. As for today's theme, make it anything about
Yosemite, but preferably Yosemite history."

Jan hardly heard Dave's usual groan. Here was her
chance to write up in theme form the material she'd been
gathering about Samuel Talmadge! She had absorbed so
much, and thought so much about him, that her pencil
went right to work. Her theme began:

"Almost everyone has heard about John Muir.
Lots of people have read about Galen Clark and
James Hutchings because they were famous men.
They were important to Yosemite history. But there
was another important Yosemite pioneer who is
not well known and should be. He was Samuel
Thompson Talmadge.

"Every time you see the rock wall around the
Yosemite Cemetery, you are looking at something
he made. Every time you climb the trail to Yosemite
Falls you are walking on a trail he helped to build.
Every time——"

Later Miss Fenton read Jan's theme out loud to the
class, praised it, and asked if she could keep it. "I'm proud
of you, Jan. You used initiative and wrote an outstanding
theme."

Dave gave her the thumbs up sign and a big grin. Even
one of the girls smiled at Jan. As for Jan herself, she felt as

if she could float out the window because she was so full of happiness.

A great storm covered the Valley floor and the cliffs above it with snow and ice during the next few days. Snow drifted three feet deep in places. Foot-long icicles hung from the eaves of the Kerns' house. Walls of snow were banked along the path that Toby and Mr. Kern had shoveled to the plowed road. When the sun shone down brilliant fingers of light on Saturday, Mrs. Kern announced, "Skiing for the menfolk, ice-skating for us gals. Come on, let's go."

Jan loved skating. She felt as if she were ten feet tall as she slid confidently around the rink. Wind reddened her cheeks, and she liked the sliding sound her skates made against the ice. Margie and her friends swooped past her, in pairs. Mother skated with Martha. The boys paired off too. Only Jan skated by herself. She didn't feel lonely, though, for many older people hailed her.

Best of all, she overheard two girls talking about a skating party. "I hope I win a prize this year," one girl said.

"Better start practicing, then. Margie Scanlon will take half of the prizes if we aren't in good shape," the other one warned.

Jan's eyes glowed. A skating party with prizes! She knew she couldn't beat anybody, especially Margie, in figure skating, but she might win a race.

Her mother glided to her side. "I'm going to the store. Keep an eye on Martha till I come back."

Contentedly Jan circled the rink with Martha until she heard Margie call loudly, "Anybody who wants a real race, follow me to the river. It's frozen for the first time in years."

A number of boys and girls slung skates over their shoulders to follow her down the road. "Let's go," Jan urged.

"No, Mother said she'd be back." Martha was the voice of authority. "Anyway, Daddy said a hundred times to stay away from the river."

"But it's frozen now," Jan protested.

Just then Margie looked back and called out in a nasty tone, "What's wrong, Miss History Know-It-All? Afraid I'll beat you? Well, you're right."

Martha changed her mind instantly. "Come on, Jan. You've got to race Margie. You can beat her!"

8 DISASTER

IT WAS AMAZING to Jan that ice could imprison the Merced. Boys threw rocks to test the ice's thickness. It held. Skates were buckled on. A course was chosen and two girls in red clothing were selected to mark the finish line. Some of the boys cleared off tree branches and pine cones. Five children elected to race, and Jan was one of them. All the other children crowded onto the thick ice on the river's edge so they could watch.

Jan looked up at snow-mantled Half Dome, so mighty and so indifferent to human beings. Next summer, she vowed, after the snow had melted, she would climb the modern cableway to the top. That made her think of Florence Hutchings. How would she have felt about the race?

"Don't change your mind, Jan," Margie sneered. "You can win fifth place."

Jan forgot history, Martha, everything, except a consuming desire to beat Margie Scanlon.

"On your mark, get set, GO!"

Margie took the lead immediately, but Jan skated hard and smoothly and caught up. The red figures loomed closer. Cheers resounded. Jan's heart pounded and she was gasping for air, but Margie was no longer ahead of her. Instead, the girls were even. In a final effort, Jan inched ahead. The heady knowledge that she could win spurred her on.

"JAN!" There was terror in Martha's scream.

Jan skidded, pivoted, and raced back with every ounce of speed she could summon. She was going so fast that the knot of children blurred. Out a ways there was a dark spot. Martha's head! She had fallen through the ice!

"I'm coming, Martha!" she called breathlessly. She saw her sister's head go under, then come back up. "Tread water," Jan commanded. "Dog paddle."

In a flurry of awkward movements, she stopped, unbuckled her skates and eased herself down. "Somebody bring me a long branch quick. Hurry!"

A choking sound came from Martha before the water closed over her head again.

Jan flattened herself on the ice and began inching toward the break. Someone gripped her by the ankles. The ice cracked ominously. Martha came back up, arms flailing wildly.

"Dog paddle." Jan's voice was thin, tense. The ice sagged slightly. She stopped, still a good five feet from her terror-stricken sister. Someone slithered a branch past her. Jan caught at it and held it tightly. Martha grabbed it, and as it bent with her weight, more ice broke off. The water was dark and ugly, deep and frightening.

"Hold on, Martha, and we'll pull you out." Jan began to inch backward, the hands holding her ankles pulling her slowly. The ice cracked. Jan's elbow went through. The cold of the water shocked her. "Pull," she whispered hoarsely, and felt herself moving back. Martha moved through the water, choking with swallowed water but holding grimly to the branch.

When she hit the ice her body broke it, but Jan was back on more solid ice. "Now really yank," commanded some-one—it sounded like Margie. "Jan has to pull Martha up onto the solid part."

Jan's fear now was that the branch would break. She pulled on it steadily, her wrists and arms aching. Finally Martha's head and shoulders came up over the solid ice. Jan pulled again, and Martha slid clear up. Margie caught Martha by the shoulder, then slid her further forward. She began artificial respiration as Jan staggered to her feet. Martha coughed up what seemed like buckets of water. Jan staggered to her feet, not sure of what to do next. All she could think of was that Martha was alive. She was miserable but alive. Jan wanted to hug her.

The quiet that had held for so long was broken. "Here come the rangers!" a shout went up.

They came on the run. Three of them. They relieved Margie and wrapped Martha in blankets. "Where are you taking me?" she cried out. "I want my mother. I want Jan."

Jan stepped to her side. One of the rangers explained, "We're taking you straight to the doctor so he can make sure you didn't swallow the whole Merced River." The ranger scooped up Martha and added, "After that we'll take you home. Where's your mother?" he asked Jan.

"At the store."

"I want Jan to come," Martha choked.

A new voice answered. "In just a few minutes, she'll follow you. First I want to ask her some questions."

"Jan saved me," Martha called back. "She's brave."

"Now," boomed Superintendent Scanlon's voice, "what happened? Why are you children on the river? You know it isn't safe."

The group was silent. Jan hadn't known the river was

"Jan saved me," Martha said. "She's brave."

forbidden territory even when it was frozen. "We came over to have a race," she admitted.

"All of you? No wonder the ice broke."

"Just five of us until Martha screamed. Then we all tore back to help her." Suddenly Jan remembered what Merced meant. Today it hadn't been any "Lady of Mercy."

The superintendent was grim as he spoke. "Marjory, you and all of you resident children know you are never to be on the river ice, let alone skate, unless it's been frozen for days and there is adult supervision." He elaborated sternly a while, then ended his admonitions, "A child almost drowned because of your disobedience. Go straight home and tell your parents what you have done. You too, Marjory. I'll talk to you later."

Margie, white-faced and quiet, stumbled off with Alice. Jan swallowed, and her voice came out thready. "Thanks for helping, Margie, thanks a lot."

Superintendent Scanlon escorted Jan to his car. "You're pretty wet. I'll take you straight home for a change of clothes."

"Are you going to talk to my mother?"

"Not now, but relax, Jan, for when I do, I'm going to tell her she has a very brave and resourceful little girl."

Jan was still warmed by his unexpected praise when he let her off at the shoveled-out pathway. Smoke was drifting out of the stovepipe. Martha and Mother must be home. Her steps lagged. Mother wouldn't say she was brave. Even though she was cold, Jan shoveled some snow off the front steps, then swept them carefully. Next she stacked stove wood high up on her arms. At last, her reasons for delay used up, she called, "Please open the door," and walked in to dump her armload in the woodbox.

One glance at Mother's face and she knew she was in for it. "You were certainly in a tearing rush to come in the house." Mrs. Kern was sarcastic. "Took you six minutes by the clock."

Jan bit her lip hard to keep from crying. "Oh, Mother, I know Martha almost drowned. I know I shouldn't have gone to the river and raced. I was so scared."

"Jan." Mother's arm went around her. "Have you stopped to think that you might have gone through the ice too? Both of you might have drowned. Oh, I can't think of it." Tears welled in her eyes, and she hugged Jan hard.

"But I had to help Martha. I had to."

"Of course you did. It just terrifies me to think how close I came to losing you both." Mother's voice was husky. "You're sopping wet. Dry yourself and climb into some fresh, warm clothes. And Jan darling, I'm proud of you, and your father will be proud too."

Martha was sleeping in their room under a pile of blankets, so Jan tiptoed into the bathroom to towel herself dry, then pull on clean, warm jeans and a long-sleeved flannel shirt. Both the superintendent and Mother were upset, but Mother was proud of her. This knowledge warmed Jan more than the dry clothes or the cup of hot cocoa Mrs. Kern gave her when she went back into the big room.

Jan looked around at the house, which she had hated so at first. Daddy had painted the big all-purpose kitchen-living room a light yellow. The old wood range rumbled in one corner, Mother and Daddy's double bed was in another; then there was the round dining room table and storage cupboards. It was a friendly room. Jan always felt good in it, especially now that Martha was safe and Mother was in a forgiving mood.

"Why don't you visit the hospital, Jan? The nurse who helped with Martha knew you and asked me to send you over so you could see firsthand why the hospital needs a new wing," Mother said, after Jan had finished her cocoa and relaxed. "Be back before dark, though. I've had enough worries for one day."

Quickly, Jan buckled on her snow boots and shouldered into a jacket.

Visiting the hospital was exciting. It had an antiseptic, foreign odor and was strangely quiet. A nurse showed her the rooms. There weren't very many, but all the beds were full.

"On a weekend like this when people are skiing at Badger Pass," the nurse explained, "and somebody sprains or breaks something, we have to put them in the hallway. See? There are two injured skiers behind those screens. They came in this afternoon with injuries, and there's no other place for them today. Your sister had only emergency treatment; otherwise she would have had to stay in the hall."

"Good grief!" Jan sputtered, "it'd be bad enough to be in the hospital, but it would be horrible to be right here with people walking past!"

It wasn't dark when Jan went back outdoors. Just cold. Cold enough so that she ran into the store, to walk through it and warm up.

The Village store was almost empty of customers. It had little business in the winter except for the residents, because the snow kept campers away. Other Park visitors, mainly skiers, stayed in the hotels and didn't need to buy groceries.

"Hello, Jan." Ginny Carruthers' mother was one of the checkers. "How about a doughnut to warm you up?"

"Great idea. Thanks." Mrs. Carruthers never let Jan go away without a doughnut or a cookie.

"Ginny tells me that you saved Martha's life today."

Jan swallowed. That story had spread fast. Several shoppers were looking at her curiously. "It was a dumb thing to do," she muttered.

Ginny's mother was shocked. "To save her?"

Jan couldn't help blushing. "No, to let her on the river in the first place. Say, remember you said you'd like to give ten dollars to the hospital fund?"

"Yes. Some day, I said. Probably after Christmas."

Jan was relieved to have the subject changed, and eagerly told Mrs. Carruthers about the overcrowded hospital. "How would you like to give a dollar a week until ten weeks are gone? Wouldn't that be easier than giving ten dollars all at once?"

Mrs. Carruthers considered, then bent down behind the counter to pick up her purse and handed Jan a dollar. "There you are," she said.

"I like that idea too." Jan recognized the other woman as a ranger's wife. "I'll give you fifty cents a week because my husband is giving too."

Jan collected $2.50 more and a bag of doughnuts before she left the store, pleased with the pay-each-week plan. On impulse she stopped at the soda fountain and explained the plan and the need for a new hospital wing. One of the men loaned her paper and pencil to write down the names and amounts of all those who donated. She pocketed four more dollars and a quarter, promising to give out receipts on Monday.

It was black outside, and she had promised to be home before dark. She ran hard, not wanting to be in any more trouble. She burst into the house red-faced and gasping for breath.

Mother was a little grim. "Jan, I asked you especially to be home before dark. There'd better be a good reason."

Jan pulled the money and the scrawled sheet from her pocket. "Collecting," she said when she caught her breath, "money for the hospital."

Mother read the paper. "What's this pay weekly business?"

Jan explained enthusiastically while she shed her jacket and boots.

"Whose idea was it?"

"Mine, and does it ever work! How much do you want to give?"

"Why, you! We have already given twenty-five dollars, but we'll match that."

Martha wandered in, clutching her piggy bank. "Can I give a nickel a week?"

Solemnly Jan wrote out the receipt, knowing that to Martha a nickel was a lot of money.

They were halfway through dinner before Mother talked about the river accident. Daddy was rather glowering-looking and made Jan promise never, never to go on the ice again without an adult. Jan promised for about the sixth time, and Daddy hugged Martha hard and held Jan's hand so she knew he wasn't angry, just upset.

Most of the day on Sunday, Jan practiced speed and figure skating. Toby had told her the skating party was slated for Friday night at the ice rink. Beating Margie in a race seemed more important than even the essay contest. Invitations would come in the mail.

9   **TRIUMPHS AND TROUBLES**

AS JAN CLIMBED out of her snow clothes in the coatroom on Monday morning, someone said casually, "Hi, Jan. Has Martha recovered from her bath in the river?"

Just that. A greeting and a casual question, but it was a girl, Alice. "Pretty good," Jan managed. "She's tough."

"So are you! See you later." Alice walked on into the classroom, leaving an open-mouthed Jan behind her.

It had been ages since any of the girls had spoken to her except to laugh at her.

"Oh—hi, Jan," another girl, whose name was Ellen, came in. "I wanted to tell you how terrific I thought you were to save your sister, but the superintendent shooed us off."

Jan hung up her jacket. "Thanks," she said. "I was scared to death."

Ellen laughed. "So was I. I was hanging onto your ankles, and I was just sure I was going to let you slip."

"You mean you were the one that held me?" Jan had thought it was one of the boys. "Wow, thanks. That was really great, especially after my elbow went through the ice."

Ellen shuddered. "That was when I closed my eyes and began to pray."

"You pulled me back just when I had to move fast," Jan assured her gratefully.

Still another girl said, "Hi, Ellen, hi, Jan. How's the great heroine today?"

It wasn't said in a mean way, Jan knew. It was just that girl's way of being friendly. "Fine," she answered, swallowing hard, and fine she was. Three girls, all friends of Margie's, had spoken to her. She hadn't realized how much their silence had hurt until it was broken. Margie ignored her, as usual, as she took her seat, but Jan didn't mind. She kept looking at the friendly girls wonderingly. Because she had tried to save Martha, they were acting differently toward her—friendly.

Miss Fenton talked to them about the dangers of the river, praised the rescuers, then said, "I have an announcement to make. Remember the essay you wrote about Mrs. Meade's father, Jan?"

Jan nodded, conscious of the whole class watching her. "Well, I liked it so much that I showed it to the editor of *Yosemite Nature Notes*, and he liked it so well that he printed it in *Yosemite Nature Notes.* Congratulations!" She handed Jan five copies of the small magazine.

Joy rose in Jan, a wonderful inner pride that her work was good enough for publication in an adult magazine even if she wasn't on the class paper. A picture of bearded Samuel Talmadge stared up at her. Beside it was the title "A Pioneer of Yesterday," by Jan Kern.

"You don't mind, do you, Jan?" Miss Fenton asked.

"Mind?" Jan stammered. "Hardly! could I run over to give one to Mrs. Meade at lunchtime? She's going to be excited too."

"That would be nice. Now, children, open your books and let's go to work."

Notes began to pass Jan's way. That wasn't unusual. She and the boys exchanged notes nearly every day. These notes were different. Three were from girls! They said that her article was great. The boys said almost the same thing, but the girls' messages meant more to Jan. She wanted to save them, so she slipped them inside her shoe.

All day long, she was in a glow with pride and happiness. Margie subtracted from it a little by making sarcastic remarks about "our great author," but Mrs. Meade's pleasure added to Jan's glow.

After school she raced home, arriving pantingly to tell her mother. "Guess what?"

Martha ran to her, sobbing, "I'm not going to the skating party either, Jan, even if I did get an invitation."

Jan let the magazines drop to the floor, her glow punctured like a balloon. "Didn't I get an invitation?"

"I'm sure there's a mistake," Mrs. Kern said. "It will come tomorrow."

"No, it won't." Tears slid slowly down Jan's cheeks. She had counted on the party, counted on another chance to beat Margie in a race. Instead Margie had beaten *her*, for Jan was positive that Margie had been responsible for her not being asked.

Mrs. Kern's sigh was loud in the silence. "Do you know why Margie and the girls don't like you?"

"Because I'm a tomboy, I guess. I don't know. I don't care."

Mother stood, her shoulders sagging just a little. "All right, but think about it, Jan. I don't want you to be unhappy."

It was snowing outside, so Jan retreated to her bedroom. Her eyes ached and she had a choking feeling down in her throat, but she didn't cry. Had the girls been nice to

It was so cold that Yosemite Falls froze, and Jan and Martha had to run to school to keep warm.

her because they knew she hadn't been invited to the party? They had said nice things about how she had rescued Martha, and then there had been the notes about the article. She shook the pieces of scratch paper from her shoe to reread them. It was hard to remember how happy they had made her so short a time ago.

"Jan darling, you didn't tell me!" Mother came running in.

"Tell you what?"

"About the article in *Yosemite Nature Notes*." Mother hugged her. "Oh, dear, I'm so proud of you I could burst! Why, the article looks so elegant—so professional—and makes fascinating reading. I'm so proud! Wait till your father sees it. He'll be proud too!"

Some of Jan's earlier excitement seeped back. "Miss Fenton turned it in, and I didn't know anything about it until this morning. Mother, girls wrote me these notes, see?"

Mrs. Kern read them intently. "Isn't this nice! Your first fan mail."

Jan hesitated, smoothing out the crumpled papers. "You don't think they wrote them because they felt sorry for me on account of being left out of the party, do you?"

"Heavens no!" Mother was emphatic. "You can tell by what they say that they're pleased for you. Why don't you try to make friends with them since they've been this nice? I'll make some ice box cookies for your lunch. You could give them some.

"All right," but Jan still wondered if they had known that she wasn't invited—wondered and worried.

In the morning Alice waved and Ellen said "Hi," and Jan felt better. Miss Fenton had another announcement to make. Jan wasn't paying much attention until she heard the hospital's name mentioned. Miss Fenton was saying, "Ranger Dunning feels we should take part in the fund-raising campaign. The whole school is to be represented by a chairman elected by this class. Nominations are now in order."

Dave stood up promptly. "I nominate Jan Kern."

"I nominate Margie Scanlon," one of the girls said.

Another railroad job, Jan thought bitterly. She remembered that there were six more girls than boys. She counted and found that three girls were absent. If she voted for herself the vote would come out fourteen to thirteen. She felt sick. They voted by raising their hands.

Miss Fenton said, in a pleased tone, "Marge eight. Jan nineteen. Congratulations, Jan, and congratulations, class. That was a fair election. You voted for what a person could do."

Jan felt stunned. Margie had lost eight to nineteen. That meant six girls had voted for her—Alice and Ellen and four others. Jan couldn't believe it. This meant she had six friends. That meant she had won. A warm feeling spread in her.

"Now, Jan," Miss Fenton said, "will you tell the class more about the fund?"

Jan began haltingly, but soon she was telling them all about the shortage of rooms at the hospital and how great the need was for a new wing. She told them how she had solicited money and explained the pay-by-the-week plan.

At noon, Jan sat near Alice and Ellen and gave them some cookies. Alice asked, "Did you make them?"

"Who, me?" Jan was taken back. "I can't even work the can opener."

"My mother's going to teach us how to make Christmas

cookies," Alice said. "You know, all different shapes. Why don't you come over tomorrow after school?"

"I'd like to." Jan was outwardly calm but inwardly excited.

"Can I come too?" Dave asked in a phony girl voice.

"Girls only," Alice said.

Girls only! And Jan Kern was one of the girls, and six girls had voted for her to be chairman. Jan felt six, twelve, eighteen feet tall—tall with happiness.

This was marred when Margie came up beside her. "I thought you didn't associate with girls."

Jan looked at her, saw the resentment in Margie's otherwise pretty face. Maybe she didn't mean to sound nasty. Maybe she was just disappointed that she hadn't been elected chairman of the fund-raising committee.

When Jan didn't answer her resentful challenge, Margie said, "My father read your article. He says you ought to be writing for our class newspaper, so I guess it's okay with me. You can be a reporter if you want." Margie's expression was sullen, her words disagreeable.

Jan tried to ignore the anger that flared in her, but she couldn't. "It may be okay with your majesty," she said hotly, "but it's not okay with me. I'm not about to become one of your subjects."

"That's fine with me." Margie was furious. " I only asked you because Dad told me to."

That did it. Jan forgot that she was on probation and remembered only that this was the girl who had made her miserable so many times.

"Your dad's an all-right guy, but you're not fit to touch a typewriter."

"Why, you short-haired tomboy," Margie sputtered vindictively, "you're nothing but a—ruffian."

Jan grabbed her by the collar. "Take that back!"

"Stop that, you two," Miss Fenton commanded sharply. "Go to the office, Jan."

As Jan dropped her hand, Margie's tongue flitted in and out. Jan gave Margie a shove that sent her sprawling and ran for the office.

Miss Fenton followed her.

"If I'm expelled," Jan asked miserably, "may I go home and tell Mother first?"

"You're not expelled," Miss Fenton said irritably, "for the simple reason that I heard most of the argument and feel that Margie's at fault too, but I am going to call your mother."

Jan gripped the desk. "No. Oh, please stop dialing. I'll be so good you won't know me. I'll—"

"Never mind the promises," Miss Fenton said dryly. "I've heard them all before. Mrs. Kern? Cherry Fenton at school. There's been some trouble here between Jan and Margie. The skating party? She wasn't? I didn't know that. Yes. If you would come over after school."

Following the conversation had been agony for Jan. Mother was coming, and Miss Fenton would tell her everything. "Do I stay after school too?"

"No, I need to talk to your mother alone. Maybe she can help us all. I hadn't known, for instance, that you weren't invited to the skating party. Now go back to class, and don't let me catch you even looking at Margie."

When Jan walked back into the room, the class was silent. She wanted to turn and run. "Come on," Dave half-growled. "Nobody's going to eat you."

"You're too tough." Jan stared. That was Alice, and she was smiling shyly.

She went to her desk, feeling about two and a half feet

high. Margie glared at her, but Jan was careful to ignore her. Despite the reassurance that she hadn't lost her friends, the afternoon dragged by. If only Mother weren't coming. If only she didn't have to know. What would Miss Fenton say? What would Mother do? What would Daddy say? She made so many mistakes in her arithmetic that she had to copy it over twice.

10 GIRL FRIENDS

AFTER SCHOOL Jan exercised Tioga, trying not to think about her mother listening to Miss Fenton and hearing about her outburst at school. As she rode past Mrs. Meade's house the old lady hailed her.

"How do you feel today, Miss Historian?"

Tioga whinnied, so Jan's mumble went unheard.

"Would you go to the store for me, please? Here's a list of things I need."

Jan was glad to escape Mrs. Meade's searching gaze. At the store she was delayed by two women who wanted to contribute to the hospital fund. When she returned with the groceries, Mrs. Meade met her outside.

"No, no, don't dismount, just hand the package to me. Your mother was here looking for you. You'd better hustle that horse to the stable and make tracks for home." Her seamed old face was troubled. "I'm sorry if I have added to your troubles, child."

Even hurrying, it took Jan half an hour to ride Tioga to the stable, rub him down, and run all the way home.

When she entered the house, her mother was rolling out pie dough. Mrs. Kern's voice was flat. "It was nice of you to shop for Mrs. Meade."

Jan waited for rebuke, for anger. When the silence lengthened, she burst out, "Go ahead and say it."

"Say what? That I am terribly disappointed that you didn't confide your troubles to me?"

Again there was a heavy silence. Jan unzipped her jacket. "You mean I should have told you about the probation?"

"That and the reasons behind it." Her tone was grim. "Parents are to help, Jan, and you haven't given your father and me a chance."

Mother's attitude confused Jan. She had expected her to be angry; instead she was sad and almost sweet. "Why, Jan, why?"

"I don't know how to tell you," she hesitated, "except the girls never liked me because I'm a tomboy. Some of them feel differently now. Alice asked me to her house after I gave her some of your cookies."

"Fine. And Miss Fenton told me that you were elected chairman of the fund-raising committee, so some of the girls did vote for you."

"Six of them," Jan remembered proudly.

After dinner, when Mother started to tell Tom Kern, he said sternly, "I think you have some explaining to do, young lady."

"That's the whole difficulty." Calmly Mother followed them into the girls' bedroom. "Jan refuses to be a young lady. She resists being a girl, and she has been causing trouble at school."

"Jan! How?"

"Showing off. Fighting with Margie Scanlon." In the talk and explanation that followed, Jan felt more and more miserable with each question.

When she was so weary that tears ran down her cheeks,

her father suddenly hugged her. "Life sure gets compli-
cated, doesn't it, honey? You look up 'tomboy' and 'show-
off' in the dictionary and see if you wouldn't rather be Jan
Kern, a girl. That would suit me just fine."

Jan was left in her room with the dictionary. She already knew what tomboy meant, a girl acting like a bois-
terous boy. The definition of show-off was worse. It meant
"to make a display of . . . to behave in a manner intended
to attract attention." Thoughtfully, Jan closed the book.
Yes, she had been a show-off; so had Margie and so had
Florence Hutchings. She had shown off by wearing men's
clothes, rolling and smoking cigarettes, and tearing
through the Valley on horseback.

An image of the dead girl's unhappy face popped into
Jan's mind. Looking in the mirror, she saw another unhappy expression. Her lower lip stuck out sullenly, her
blue eyes were rebellious and there were frown lines in
her forehead. T-squares and plumb bobs, what an ugly
girl! she thought.

She grabbed a comb and tried to make her short pieces
of hair hide her ears. That Jan in the mirror had to go!

Next morning she ran to school, only pausing long
enough to let Martha catch up with her. The cold was
intense and crept in, like an icy knife, through her heaviest
jacket. But the Valley was beautiful—still and white, with
ice and snow glittering in the frigid air. Yosemite Falls was
frozen ice, plastered like a giant Christmas tree against the
granite cliffs. Snow-mantled trees marched along the tops
of the canyon, looking like tiny white statues.

Alice met them as they raced into the hall. "Isn't it
terrific? My father says it's the coldest December in years.
You're coming this afternoon, aren't you, Jan?"

The renewal of the invitation made her feel wanted. "Sure," she said, "but don't blame me if the cookies turn out like lumps of clay. I'd like to have you be on the fund-raising committee with me. Will you?"

"Sure. I'd really love to work. My dad's a doctor there, you know."

"Honest?" Jan's surprise was genuine. "Then you should be chairman."

Alice had long, dark hair and a nice freckled smile. "Oh, no. I didn't know as much about the hospital as you do until I talked to my father last night."

Just as the bell rang, Alice said, awkwardly, "I'll see what I can do about the Christmas dance. Margie needn't think she runs everything around here."

There wasn't time to ask about the dance, but Jan knew, from the way Alice acted, it must have an invitation committee such as the skating party had had. She could dance a little. Daddy and Toby and Mother practiced sometimes. Hurriedly, she made her way to her desk. From now on she had to be good even if it hurt.

At noontime she invited the two girls, Dave, and the right fielder to be on the committee. They all accepted eagerly. Jan felt that she had a representative committee except for one thing. She had put off approaching one last member. Reluctantly she walked over to Margie, who gave her a glaring look.

Jan wanted to retreat right then, but she had thought it all through the night before. "I'm hoping you'll serve on the fund-raising committee," she said, and her voice sounded odd in her own ears.

"Why should I?" Margie's voice was pitched low because Miss Fenton was nearby.

Aloud, and steadily, Jan said, "If the drive is to be a

success, we need everyone to help, and the editor of the class newspaper has more power than any of the others."

"In that case," Margie, far from gracious, said "I guess I'll be on your dumb old committee."

Jan was thinking angrily that if that was the way young ladies acted, she'd stay a tomboy forever. As she started back to her own desk, she heard Margie audibly stage-whisper, "That's just her way of trying to snag an invitation to the Christmas dance."

That was mean and untrue. Jan swung around, opened her mouth, then shut it again, remembering just in time that she was on probation.

"Sometimes, class, I see and hear things that startle me," Miss Fenton said in a calm but tight voice. "Jan pleased me with her self-control, and your little speech disgusted me, Margie."

There was nothing Margie could say. She just glowered, and when she frowned that way, she wasn't a bit pretty. She looked as ugly as Jan had the previous night. Jan was glad that Miss Fenton had overheard. She was gladdest of all because she had had sense enough to sit down before she'd caused further trouble.

That afternoon Alice's mother welcomed her warmly. "We're so glad you could come, Jan. Alice speaks of you often, and my husband says you are one of the best fund-raisers for the hospital."

Ellen was the only other girl there, and they spent two hours busily learning how to make Christmas cookies. Alice's mother was patient with them, praising their efforts. Jan was surprised at how good her cookies tasted and how much fun she was having with just a couple of girls. Afterwards they sprawled in the living room before the fireplace, talking. They discussed the essay contest because Miss Fenton had reminded them again of the deadline for entries.

"I've been doing some reading at the research library," Ellen said, "but haven't picked my subject. What are you going to write about, Alice?"

"I don't think I'll tell," Alice answered hesitantly. "Too many of us might write about the same topic. Not that I don't trust you two—I just think it would be better if it's a secret."

"I wish I'd started earlier," Ellen complained. "Most of the Yosemite reference books are checked out, and the museum is full of kids looking at the historical exhibits."

"The trouble is," Alice said, putting another log on the crackling fire, "Margie can really write, and her dad knows all the history. Jan, maybe you can win first prize."

"Me? I'll try because I want to win for myself, but I thought Margie was your friend."

"She was—is, but she's always so superior, and we had a fight about—never mind."

Jan guessed that the fight had been about the skating party and herself. She wanted to tell them she was glad that they were her friends, but she didn't know how.

Ellen said, "You know there's a skating competition Saturday too, Jan. Kids come from places like Mariposa, Fresno, and Merced to enter. If you could just beat Margie in the speed race, it'd be as good or better than if you win the trophy at her party."

Jan decided immediately that she would beat Margie, even if she fell through the ice trying. She hated to leave, but seeing the clock, she said, "I have to go or I'll be late meeting the school bus. Toby will never believe I baked these cookies myself."

She was halfway down the shoveled walk, when she whirled and ran back. "I didn't say thank you," she said, opening the door a crack, "I really had a wonderful time. Thanks."

She made a hasty stop to give Mrs. Meade some of her cookies. "Why, Jan, I'm overwhelmed. If you and your friends want to come over during Christmas vacation, I'll show you how to make old-fashioned taffy. You might be able to sell some for the fund."

Jan hugged her impulsively. "That's a keen idea, and I wonder about making wreaths. Do you think that would go over?"

"It certainly should, but where are you going to find evergreens? You can't cut branches of trees—not in a national park."

"I know, and I won't," Jan answered. "My dad says that lots of little trees, mostly cedars, have to be cleared this week for a new parking area."

"In that case," Mrs. Meade said, "I want a big wreath, please."

Jan raced off to meet the bus, full of ideas and plans to tell the boys and with good memories of an afternoon with the girls.

Saturday Jan woke up with a sore throat. She knew she should tell her mother, but then she wouldn't be able to race that afternoon. She had to race. Had to. When Mrs. Kern asked at breakfast how she felt, Jan lied. "Fine."

When she went to practice skating, her throat felt raw; and by the time she came back for lunch, her eyes were weepy and she couldn't hold back a sneeze.

"Into bed with you, young lady," her mother said, after looking carefully at her.

"Not until after the race, Mother, please. I have to be in the race."

Mrs. Kern felt her forehead. "Bed" was the verdict. "I'm sorry about the race, honey, but I don't want you to have pneumonia. A cold is bad enough." She saw that Jan changed into pajamas, was warmly covered, and swallowed some pills. Then she left some juice and the radio on the bedside table.

"Now if you're comfortable, the rest of us will go to Badger Pass and cheer Toby on in his skiing competition. Okay?" Mrs. Kern asked.

"I'll be all right." Jan blew her nose, then reached for her notebook. "I'll work on my essay." Her thought was that if she couldn't beat Margie skating, maybe she could beat her writing.

Soon she forgot all about that and became absorbed in her subject, "Yosemite Tomboys," and their love of freedom and the Park.

There had been three well-known tomboys—Florence Hutchings, Frankie Crippen, and Mrs. Meade, when she was young. None of them had been afraid of tackling anything, from swimming the Merced River in its spring turbulence to ascending Half Dome aided only by a rope. It was Jan's ambition to make that climb too, but she was glad that there were two steel cables to hang on to now. Florence Hutchings had been a daredevil tomboy to the end of her short life, but "Frankie" Crippen had reverted into Fannie, who played the piano and became a young lady.

And Mrs. Meade had tired of being a tomboy. Jan read the notes she had taken earlier. Mrs. Meade had said, "My brag was that I could do anything a boy could do, and my father said, 'Fine, you can help me shovel snow and cut wood.' You know, I got so I hated the sight of a shovel and was ashamed of my calloused hands."

"I decided maybe I'd be a girl so I wouldn't have to work so hard. Pretty soon I began liking to cook and sew and just being a girl."

Jan thought of Toby's daily chores. Before school he had to fill the woodbox and help shovel snow off the path, or spread dirt on the ice so no one would slip. After he finally arrived home on the school bus, he and Daddy cut wood and refilled the woodbox. Sometimes Toby climbed on the porch roof to shovel off snow that might crush it. If the pipes froze, Toby had to help Daddy carry water from the river.

Her own chores of table setting and putting out the trash seemed pleasant and easy in contrast. Maybe, she thought drowsily, being a girl wasn't so bad after all.

11 WREATH MAKING

WHEN JAN woke up she began sneezing, and Mrs. Meade called from the other room, "That's too loud to be a snore, so I guess you're awake."

"What are you doing here?" Jan's voice came out a hoarse croak. She had a cold, all right.

"Working on a quilt and keeping an ear out for you," the old lady said cheerfully, "but I won't come in unless you need me. A cold can be pretty serious to a body that's lived as long as I have."

"I missed the race," Jan croaked mournfully.

"And the grave," Mrs. Meade said with spirit. "Now I can tell you about the time that McCauley started the firefall that became so famous.[1] Well—"

Even though they were interesting, eventually, Mrs. Meade's stories put Jan back to sleep. Toby jolted her awake near dinnertime. "Say, Jan, you'll never guess how the three chowderheads came out."

"Did you win any races?"

---

1. The famous firefall of glowing embers, which was pushed over Glacier Point, was ended in 1968.

"Croak, croak. In one race, Chuck won, Rick was second, and I was third! How do you like that? I came in fourth and seventh in the other races, but Rick won a couple of seconds, and Chuck took third in the giant slalom. How's that for a record?"

"Terrific," Jan croaked. "Did you hear if Margie won the skating race?"

Toby leaned against the doorjamb. "Alice told me Margie came in third. Some flashy gal from Mammoth took first, and a girl from Mariposa won second."

In the morning Jan was better, although Mother made her stay in bed. She had asked Toby and Rick to collect greenery for the Christmas wreaths. Then they all worked on fashioning them. By afternoon they had twenty colorful wreaths ready to sell. The biggest and best one was for Mrs. Meade. While Jan rested, the boys went out to see how the residents liked them. When she awoke she could hear subdued conversation in the big kitchen. Toby came in answer to her hoarse call.

"Sold them all for a dollar apiece." His grin was wide and proud. " But you were right about making them all different. That's what we're trying to do now."

"Who's we?"

"Rick, Chuck, me, your whole committee, and a couple of fellows off the baseball team. Fast as we make them, the girls are going out to sell them. Martha's our best salesman. She sold seven of the twenty all by herself. This was sure a keen idea, Jan. We're going to make tons of money."

"I wish I could help." She couldn't help feeling a little left out.

"Forget it," he advised. "Mom said for you to lay off

making wreaths or she'd have to use a vacuum cleaner to clean out your bed."

Alice called, "You sound like death warmed over."

Jan couldn't think of a suitable answer but felt good that her committee members were there. Toby brought her a pencil and paper so that she could make a list of people she needed to collect from during the following week. If the wreaths kept on selling, they were going to have a big sum of money to turn in toward the hospital wing. Despite being miserable from the cold, she was happy.

While she did accounts, reports kept coming in. Toby would shout, "Just sold another eight wreaths, Boss; have to go and load up with more cedar branches."

"Did you think about checking with Superintendent Scanlon first?" Jan asked. "I was going to do that yesterday."

"Sure, but Dad already had, and we're just using the little trees that were cut to make room for the new parking area. There's tons more greenery than we can ever use. Scanlon's an okay guy. He asked about you and ordered four wreaths."

Martha was Jan's most frequent visitor. "Here's another five dollars that Ginny and I collected selling wreaths."

By the end of the long, busy afternoon, the committee had sold all the wreaths they had made.

Toby finished counting the money they had collected. "Maybe I'm crazy," he said with awe, "but the grand— and I do mean grand—total is sixty-seven dollars."

Mr. Kern had just come home from skiing. "Better let me check those figures, son. That's a lot of money."

Martha sold more Christmas wreaths than anybody else.

"Now you know what cooperation is, Jan," Mother called.

Cooperation meant working together, Jan remembered, and that's just what they'd done. Alice, and in fact Jan's whole committee, Rick, Toby, Chuck, Dave and, best of all, Martha and Ginny. They had been star salesmen, selling and delivering twenty-eight wreaths. And they had taken orders for more. Mother and Mrs. Meade had kept busy making cocoa and cookies for everybody except Jan. Mother had given her lots of juice, and some jello that slid easily down her sore throat.

"What's your quota?" Mr. Kern asked.

"The school's supposed to raise one hundred dollars."

"Then you're over," Dad said, "because you've turned in quite a bit of money on your own, haven't you?"

"Last time I counted it was eighty dollars," Jan told him happily. "How much does that make?"

"Altogether, one hundred and forty-seven dollars. Why, sweetheart, that's *wonderful!* I'm proud of you."

"I have twenty-three dollars to collect this week," she said excitedly, "and more wreaths, and then we're going to sell Christmas candy."

"Three cheers for Jan!" Daddy said. "I'd hug you only I don't want to catch your cold and sound like I have a mouthful of gravel."

Jan was growing again—growing tall with pride that she and the committee and their helpers had gone way over the quota assigned to them.

Mother asked, "How do you feel?"

"Ten feet tall," Jan answered hoarsely.

By Tuesday Mother let her go back to school. Miss Fenton announced in front of the class that they were glad to have her back. She went on to say, "Thanks to Jan and the fund-raising committee, our school has already exceeded its quota of money for the new hospital wing by over fifty dollars! All of that was raised by Jan and her committee. Isn't that neat? Now it's time for the rest of you to help the committee and raise more money. Do you think it's possible to add another fifty dollars to the present total, Jan?"

"Easy," Jan said positively, "if everybody will work. We need as many plates of Christmas candy and cookies as your mothers will help you bake or you can make. Or you can sell wreaths or just go out and ask for donations."

"See Jan at recess," the teacher urged, "to sign up for whatever you would rather do. And don't forget, the contest essays are due Friday."

Friday! This was Tuesday. Less than four days, Jan thought, alarmed, and I've barely begun.

After school there were wreaths to sell and Tioga to visit with a couple of apples. On her way home, she stopped to tell Mrs. Meade about going over the quota. She decided that she wasn't showing off since Mrs. Meade really wanted to know.

"That's fine as cream news!" Mrs. Meade congratulated Jan by serving her a piece of fresh-baked apple pie. "I recollect the first hospital we had in the Valley. If we had had a hospital and a doctor earlier, Floy Hutchings and Effie Crippen might not have died so young."

Jan smiled to herself as she savored the good pie. Most of Mrs. Meade's best stories began with "I recollect."

"Those were the good old days. I wish I'd lived here then."

"With dust ankle deep in the summer, mud all winter,

All of Mrs. Meade's best stories began "I recollect . . ."

no electricity, telephone, or indoor bathrooms? I like the good new days myself."

Jan nodded vigorously. "After living in construction camps, I don't mind inconveniences. You knew the pioneers and the Indians. Your father helped build the trails."

Mrs. Meade interrupted, "Now, now, don't get dewy-eyed about the past, child. You are living in a wonderful time, your father is helping to build modern roads, and we both live——"

"In the best place in the world," Jan finished triumphantly.

That night Jan wrote most of her essay. Her pages of notes and history books helped her with facts, and her own love of Yosemite helped her make the account interesting. She knew so much about Florence Hutchings, Fannie Crippen, and Hannah Talmadge Meade, and they were so real to her, that it was easy to write about them.

The class newspaper was given out when school began on Wednesday. There were two mimeographed pages with eight articles. Jan scanned them quickly. Two of them were about the skating party, two about the various races on Saturday, one about the contest, a long one about the coming Christmas party, and on the last page there were three lines about the hospital drive.

They read, "Yosemite Valley School is proud to announce that it has exceeded its quota in the hospital fund-raising drive. Good work, everybody."

Jan's indignation mounted until recess when she confronted Margie with the paper. "Couldn't you do better than that? Three measly lines."

Margie said sweetly, "What's wrong with them?"

"Everything." Jan was having a hard time restraining her temper. They were collecting an audience. "You didn't tell how much money we raised or how we did it or that we're still working. We're not through. That wing's going to cost several thousand dollars, you know, not one hundred and fifty dollars. And, another thing, you could have given the committee and the other kids a little credit. I'm chairman, sure, but about twenty different kids worked to raise that money, and one of them wasn't you."

"You're just jealous because you're not invited to the parties," Margie said spitefully.

Jan bit her lip. "Watch it," she said quietly, anger almost choking her.

"Watch it yourself. I'm not on probation. Why didn't you race Saturday?"

"I was sick, but I'll race you any time."

"This afternoon?" Margie was openly smug.

Jan's answer was instant. "You bet, as soon as school is out."

"I heard that, and I'll be the judge," Miss Fenton called from beyond the group of listening children.

12 THE HAPPY LOSER

USUALLY when school let out, the children scattered in a dozen directions. That afternoon they all filed out behind Jan, Margie, and Miss Fenton. Both girls had been allowed to go home at noon to pick up their skates. The winter sun held scant warmth, though the sky was clear and blue. Jan could hear kids from her class making bets. The boys were solidly behind her, but most of the girls backed Margie.

Jan was amazed to see how quickly a crowd of residents had gathered at the skating rink. She spotted Mother and Martha and, of all people, Mrs. Meade, so bundled up against the cold she could hardly move. Jan saw other friends of hers, too—two of the clerks from the store, a nurse, four rangers, and several strangers. She wondered who had spread the word. Martha, maybe?

Dave advised, "Take the turn fast and don't let up coming back. Good luck."

And Alice said, "I know you can win. You have to."

And Martha said, "I bet my whole month's allowance on you. Fifty cents."

Mother gave her a quick hug. "I wish you felt better, honey, but no matter whether you win or lose, do it like a champion."

Miss Fenton pointed out the course. "Skate to the end

of the rink, turn and come back to the line Dave is making. You are starting from scratch."

Sure enough, Dave was scratching a line on the ice with a pole.

Jan glanced around at the spectators, at the gnarled, ice-burdened apple trees, and at Half Dome, as ever impervious and commanding, towering above. What a great place, she thought, then concentrated on taking deep breaths.

Miss Fenton called loudly, "On your mark, get set, GO!"

Bent almost double, legs stroking smoothly, Jan started off fast. Margie's start was not quite as rapid, but soon she pulled even. Jan bore down, arms and legs moving, heart pumping. They made the turn in unison, skated hard back toward the finish line. Yells and shouts of encouragement resounded for both girls.

Jan was using every bit of her speed, every bit of her reserve, but it wasn't enough, and her chest hurt. Margie moved past. The shouts became a roar, and Margie slid over the finish line a good yard ahead of Jan.

Dave stopped Jan, held her up, panting, coughing, and feeling sick with disappointment. "Tough luck," he shouted in the world that was loud with noise, "but that was a great race." He unbuckled and removed her skates.

Jan was gasping for breath and, inwardly, fighting her disappointment. "Win or lose like a champion," Mother had said. The loser swallowed hard and elbowed her way into the crowd that was cheering Margie. Children drew back to let her in. The talk quieted and then stopped, so that they were surrounded by silence.

Jan stuck out her hand and said, "Congratulations, Margie. You won, and it was a good race."

"No matter whether you win or lose," Mother said, "do it like a champion."

For a horrible moment Margie just looked at Jan, ignoring her outstretched hand, but finally she put her own hand out. Jan shook it, said "Congratulations" again and backed off.

"Any time you want to race, let me know." Margie's tone was light, disdainful.

The bad situation was made worse by Martha's running up and handing Margie five dimes. "I lost my bet. There's your fifty cents."

Margie turned red, and Jan wished the ice would open up and swallow her.

Mrs. Kern saved the day by calling, "All aboard for cocoa and cookies at the Kerns' house!"

Martha, Jan, Dave, Alice, Ellen, Ginny, and two other girls crowded into the Kerns' station wagon. Mrs. Meade was already in the front seat, and in a proud, cracked soprano began singing, "For she's a jolly good fellow."

Everyone joined in heartily. When they finished singing, Jan protested, "But I lost!"

"Sure you did," Mrs. Kern said, "but you lost like a champion, and we're proud of you."

"No excuses, no tears," Dave said, "you lost big."

"I'll say," Martha muttered.

Laughter broke out, and Jan hugged Martha. She didn't know how she could feel happy after losing the race, and Martha's allowance, but she did.

At home there was cocoa with marshmallows in it for everyone, plenty of cookies, and a big cake with thick icing on it. "I had a feeling we'd need that." Mrs. Meade saw Jan's surprise.

Before they were through eating, the rest of the baseball team arrived with four girls who were on the fund-raising committee. Friendship surrounded Jan. When the food was gone, most of the crowd cleared out. Only the girls were left, she noted, astounded.

Alice cleared her throat, stammered, then said, "Now don't explode, Jan, but I was wondering if your hair couldn't be trimmed a little. It's so straggly-looking and wild."

"I think you're right, Alice." Mrs. Kern examined Jan's head critically. "Martha, bring me the scissors. With a little trimming it might look more like a girl's very short bob rather than a boy needing a haircut."

Jan saw that they were sincere. "Okay," she said, "but don't let me do it or I'll be bald again."

The girls laughed. "Good grief. I'll never forget the first time we saw you after the fire. You went around looking like you'd sock the first one who asked any questions."

Jan blushed again, then held still while her mother trimmed a piece off here and there. All the girls gave advice. When they were done, her mother brought a mirror. Jan was pleased. She looked like a girl again.

"I can hardly believe it!" Her surprise was evident.

"You mean you didn't trust us?" Alice tried to sound injured.

The kidding was friendly and fun until Martha came in. "Oh, Jan, you look like—like Jan again. Now you're pretty enough to go to the dance?"

"What dance?" Mother asked quickly.

"The Christmas party," Jan answered, just as quickly, "only I'm not going." Margie would see that no invitation was sent to her, she knew.

"How do you know?" Alice said. "The invitations don't even come out till tomorrow."

"I'm not going, though," Jan said, a little desperately,

not wanting sympathy or questions. "Say, maybe we could go collect for the fund?"

"Not today." Mrs. Kern was quite firm. "You aren't over your cold and you all earned an afternoon off. Why don't you and your friends go play?"

Play. To Jan the word meant ball. She was at a loss as to what to do with just girls.

Ellen said, "I know what. Let's have a snowball fight."

It was glorious fun to pin an enemy down with a well-aimed ball or duck one just before it would have splattered. Jan had a grand time, dodging and throwing and laughing. She was sorry when it was time for the girls to go home. She hadn't dreamed they could have such fun together.

When Toby came home, he whistled approvingly at Jan's appearance. "Hey, you look like a girl again. What an improvement!"

"Did you hear that I lost in a skating race with Margie?"

"Sure. Dave met me at the bus." Toby grabbed a last piece of cake. "But he said you were a good loser and Margie was a poor winner."

So Jan had to be content with second best, but she had the friendship and affection showered on her by family and friends. The mirror no longer reflected a sullen tomboy, but instead a happy girl. Even when she thought about not being able to attend the Christmas party, her mirrored expression managed to stay pleasant.

13 YOUNG LADY OF YOSEMITE

FOOTSTEPS pounded after Jan as she ran from school on Thursday. She was trying to struggle into her jacket at the same time and fell sprawling on the snow.

Dave helped her up. "What's wrong with you?" he asked crossly. "I'm all out of breath from chasing you."

Jan couldn't help laughing. "I was afraid I'd be stopped, and I simply have to work on my essay this afternoon or it won't be ready to turn in tomorrow."

"Well, look." Suddenly Dave seemed flustered, awkward. He swallowed hard. "Well, I was chasing you because—well, how about going to the Christmas party with me?"

Quickly, Jan knelt to rebuckle her snow boot. She didn't want Dave to see the tears in her eyes. Dave wanted her to go with him. Her first date!

"Of course, if somebody already invited you or you don't want to go with me, why—that's all right."

Jan looked up astonished. Dave was disappointed. He really wanted her to go, she could tell from his face. "Oh, I'd like to go with you," she answered truthfully, "but I won't be invited."

Dave grinned and started rolling a snowball. "Oh, yes you will be, and you are! I had a little talk with Miss

Scanlon. I told her that if you weren't invited, three-fourths of the school would not be at the party." He threw swiftly. "You'll receive an invitation."

Jan ducked his snowball and ran. "Thanks, Dave."

"Forget it," he called after her gruffly.

But Jan knew she would never forget this first invitation. Never. She was actually going to a party with a boy, and he had pressured Margie into asking her. It seemed as if she flew the rest of the way to Mrs. Meade's.

Mrs. Meade answered her last-minute questions about Yosemite tomboys carefully, and told her about a camping trip her family had made with Galen Clark.

"Satisfy an old woman's curiosity before you go." Her brown eyes twinkled as they searched Jan's face. "What makes you so happy that you're glowing today?"

Jan felt the red flood her cheeks. "Dave asked me to go to the Christmas party with him."

"No wonder you glow. You two will make a handsome couple."

"Thanks," Jan said, grinning.

As she glanced up at the canyon walls while on her way home, Jan thought of the essay prize. A week's trip in the high Sierra! Right now the wilderness above the Valley gleamed white and inhospitable. In July she knew its ways would be grassy green, flowery, and welcoming.

She added to and then rewrote her essay with new intentness, wanting it to be expressive and factual—to be first class in every way. Her pencil paused. More than any prize, she thought, she wanted to be proud of her account. She wanted Mrs. Meade to read about herself, Fannie Crippen, and Florence Hutchings, nod her white head, and say, "Jan, it's all true. That's just the way our lives were."

With that in mind, Jan reread her last paragraph, scratched it out, consulted her notes, and went on working to improve the wording.

"Jan. Telephone," Mother interrupted her later.

Jan hated to take time out to answer it. "Hello?"

"Hi, Jan, this is Rick. Will you go to the Christmas party with me?"

The magic words that meant belonging again. Jan couldn't help being thrilled, and Rick—he was older. "I'd like to, Rick, but Dave already asked me."

"Oh, heck! He sure didn't waste any time. Save me some dances, will you?"

Jan promised and hung up. She turned around to face her startled family. "You turned Rick down?" Toby couldn't believe it. "T-squares and plumb bobs, I thought you'd want to go with him! You're old friends."

"Dave asked me first, and we're friends too."

"That's fine, Jan," Mother said warmly. "We'll have to be thinking about dresses."

"Dresses?" Jan looked and sounded blank.

"You don't think you're going to wear jeans, do you?"

She was nearly through with her revision when Toby carried the Kerns' old typewriter into the bedroom. "Now what?" she groaned.

"Now I'm going to do my good deed for the day and type your old essay."

"Toby, honest?" Jan was thrilled. It would save her hours of work. Mother ignored their bedtime. Jan worked with a pencil, making minor corrections against the steady clatter of the typewriter. It was after eleven o'clock when they finally fell into bed.

Christmas vacation began with a sparkly procession of

brilliant days and icy nights. Thick marshmallowy snow rested on Clouds Rest. Only the sheer granite face of Half Dome was clear of snow. Everything—everywhere—was white.

For Jan, vacation meant time to make and sell Christmas candy, cookies, and wreaths, aided by her committee. It meant afternoons on the skating rink or sliding down hills on sleds. It meant fun and excitement. It meant belonging. Toby, Rick, and Chuck had jobs at the Badger Pass Ski Area, but she didn't really miss them. There were too many things for her to do with Alice and Ellen and other friends.

It snowed hard the night of the Christmas party. Dave came for Jan. "Dad drove me over in the snowplow so we'll be sure to make it through the drifts." A happy grin brightened his dark face. He was wearing a twin to Toby's outfit—gray flannel slacks, a white shirt, a tie, and a dark corduroy jacket. Both boys looked handsome.

"Can't I see anything but your coat?" Dave queried.

Jan laughed. "It's hiding my jeans." She held her coat wide so he could see the pretty light-blue party dress.

Dave whistled.

Outside the night was thick with snowflakes. At school they talked excitedly to friends as they took off their snow gear. When Margie came in with a strange boy, Jan said tentatively, "Hi, Margie."

Margie turned, rustling in a taffeta dress, and smiled coolly, but did not answer.

"Down girl!" Dave pressed Jan's hand warningly.

"Don't worry," Jan assured him. "She doesn't bother me, but I can't like her. Just look at the room!"

Evergreens, balloons with Santa Claus faces, colored lights, and an enormous Christmas tree had transformed the school's multi-purpose room. There was a three-piece orchestra, and Mrs. Craig was at a piano playing dance music interspersed with carols.

Even as she was swung onto the polished floor, Jan was looking around for Superintendent Scanlon. "When do you suppose the contest winner will be announced?"

"At nine o'clock," Dave answered. "Stop thinking about that or I'll step on your foot!"

As a matter of fact, she stepped on his twice before she managed to get into the rhythm. It was fun. Her face flushed happily, her eyes sparkled, and her skirt swirled out. Boys cut in. Toby, Rick, and some of the boys on the team danced with her until Dave announced, "Hey, I brought you to this party, and I'll be your partner."

At nine o'clock, Mrs. Craig played a fanfare on the piano. The dancers cleared the floor and lined up against the walls as Superintendent Scanlon stepped out beside the Christmas tree. Miss Fenton followed him, holding several envelopes.

"I am delighted to announce prizes for the historical essay contest," the big man began. "There were so many fine entries that the judges awarded a second and third prize of three days at three of the High Sierra camps, too. But I bet no one feels like leaving at the moment! The latest report I received was that there's already nine feet of snow at Tuolumne Meadows."

Scattered chuckles broke out at the thought of camping in snow like that. Jan was quiet, her mouth and throat dry.

"All right, I'll end the suspense after a few hundred more words." He grinned at the laughter. "Seriously, I want to make some remarks. Forty-two students in the fifth, sixth, seventh, and eighth grades turned in entries. All forty-two of you used the historical resources of the library and museum. Some of you re-examined the historic sites in this wonderful Valley, such as the cemetery and Galen Clark's home site, but only two of you had the extra initiative and imagination to do original research."

The room was hushed. Jan drew in her breath. She had done original research. Who else had? Margie? Dave was gripping Jan's hand until it hurt.

"Two of you went to the trouble to interview oldtimers and to check what they said against records. Those two won first and third prizes. First prize of one week's vacation at May Lake, Glen Aulin, Vogelsang——"

"Dad!" a familiar voice protested, quietly but audibly.

Superintendent Scanlon burst out laughing. "That agonized tone stops me from naming further delightful camps. First prize is proudly awarded to an essay called 'Yosemite Tomboys of Yesterday' by——"

Before he could say her name, heads were turning toward Jan. "Congratulations!" Dave roared at the same moment the superintendent said "Jan Kern!"

The room went wild. Cheers resounded. Chords boomed from the piano, and Dave swung Jan clear into the air.

"Third prize . . . third prize"—eventually quiet reigned—"goes to the other person who thought of going to our living pioneers. And, Dave, if your writing was as good as your ideas you would have won second prize. For his essay on 'Our Indian Pioneers,' third prize is awarded to David Brown."

"There must be a mistake!" Dave shouted as tumult broke out anew.

Jan hugged him. "Oh, no, there isn't!"

When the excitement died down, Superintendent Scanlon resumed speaking. "Second prize, I'm proud to say,

Everyone cheered when the winners were announced.

goes to my daughter, Marjorie Scanlon, for her work on Galen Clark. Will the three prize winners come forward?"

Applause continued as they walked up, accepted handshakes and stiff envelopes, and smiled happily. Then they all congratulated one another. Margie even shook Jan's hand. When dance music swept everyone back on the floor, Margie whisked off in her father's arms.

Jan had other ideas on her mind. "Who did you interview?"

"Chief Tom and my two oldest relatives," Dave said. "Why?"

"Could I talk to them? Did they go to the Yosemite School, and where did they live?"

"But the contest is over." Dave sounded amazed.

"My interest in Yosemite history isn't over," Jan assured him. "I want to know lots more about the people and places. Where, for instance, was the first school, and when did it begin?" She pressed her forehead against an icy windowpane. Outside, snow was still piling up in the best place in the world. She belonged to Yosemite and to herself, a girl named Jan Kern.

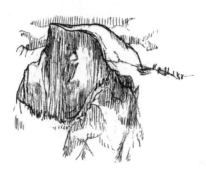

Half Dome